Wilkinsburg High School

Century of Learning, 1911-2011

One Hundred Years
at
747 Wallace Avenue
Wilkinsburg, PA

Wilkinsburg Historical Society

Wilkinsburg High School
Century of Learning, 1911-2011
is dedicated to

Professor William C. Graham
Principal 1903 - 1928
Superintendent 1929 - 1941
"He set the standard"

This book is also dedicated to the students,
alumni, faculty, staff, superintendents, and school directors
who brought honor and fame to
Wilkinsburg High School

ISBN# 978-1-4507-6082-9
Printed in the United States of America

Dedication...ii

Table of Contents...iii

Foreword...iv

Acknowledgments...v

Poems...vi

Chapter 1 - The Early Years, 1840-1910.. 1

Chapter 2 - High School Building and Dedication, 1911.........................13

Chapter 3 - Champions, Additions and Traditions, 1912-1929...............27

Chapter 4 - Athletics and Academics, 1930-1949.....................................47

Chapter 5 - WHS moves up in status, 1950-1969.....................................73

Chapter 6 - Cafeterias, Computers and Clubs, 1970-1989.......................115

Chapter 7 - Pride, Progress and Partnerships, 1990-2010.......................147

Chapter 8 - The next century begins, 2011..161

Foreword

This is an age of innovation. The world is constantly demanding something new, and it is dissatisfied unless its demands are heeded. Such a condition, however, is really beneficial to an age. The lack of such desire causes a nation or even a school to decline and lose its vigor and progressiveness.

This spirit has led Wilkinsburg High School to make many great strides in the past few years: We are now practically a self-governing student body; our activities are controlled by students and our publications are issued by students. Publications, you ask! Certainly, the "Review" and the "Year Book," the latter being the latest innovation. For many years, the demand for such a book has been pressing; now comes the realization of that demand. Though this book may not be perfect, experience will teach later editors and we shall all look forward to developments not only of the year book, but also of the democratic spirit and feeling which have done so much to advance our school.

In issuing this volume, we hope to strengthen the bonds of fellowship among the students of Wilkinsburg High and foster the ties which bind the alumni to our school. We aim to have this book reflect, in a true light, the life of the school and to keep alive the precious memories and intimate friendships of our high school days.

Acknowledging the aid our teachers and friends have given us, we send forth this book in the hope that it will accomplish well its mission and as a friend, will, in the future, bring to everyone such thoughts as memory alone would be powerless to produce. This has been our trust. We present our attempt at its fulfillment.

The Editors
1921 "Review"

In this ever-changing world, it is little wonder that we soon forget many of our past achievements, successes, friendships, and the happiness of innumerable days gone by. Let us not forget the happiness we shared in Wilkinsburg High, nor what our high school days meant to us. Choosing as our theme High Spots of WHS, we have tried to bring back many delightful memories to you, the reader. We have tried to tell the story of the opportunities - scholastic, social, and physical - which our school has offered us. We hope our book will remind you of many a happy moment spent in high school. So here they are - the High Spots of WHS.

The Editors
1939 Annual

Acknowledgments

We would like to thank the students, advisors and faculty from the past 100 years who created the Review, the Wil-Hi-Scan, the Annual, the Hi-Ways and the Tiger's Paw. It is from these student publications that excerpts and photographic images have been collected to create this centennial celebration of Wilkinsburg High School. The student publications that were studied for this centennial book have provided a record of the past century of WHS life.   We have included informal snapshots of high school life, together with more formal photographs of important events that have taken place over the years. Most of the text and captions are just as the students themselves wrote them. We have tried to preserve their own words with only minor changes for clarification. It is impossible to include every significant event, as there are hundreds of thousands of events that were important in the lives of WHS students.

Many thanks also to the School Board members for their encouragement, to Superintendent Archie Perrin for his assistance, to Joel Minnigh of the Wilkinsburg Public Library and Rian Crothers of the Wilkinsburg School Library for lending their archives for this project. Thanks are due to Jean Dexheimer of the School Board for her editing expertise and William Zimpleman for searching through Annuals for information. Special thanks to James B. Richard for sharing his vast knowledge of the Wilkinsburg Schools and for locating photos to be included, and to Anne Elise Morris for compiling the images and information in the computer. Thanks also to Richard Muzzey of Wonday Studio Photography for assistance with the photographs. We also appreciate the technical advice and guidance of Thomas Gentile of the Western Pennsylvania School for the Deaf, who provided the printing and binding of this book.

We hope that those who attended Wilkinsburg High School will enjoy the memories, learn something new about WHS, and feel a sense of 'Tiger Pride' while reading *Wilkinsburg High School: Century of Learning 1911-2011.*

Members of the Wilkinsburg Historical Society

The Wilkinsburg Historical Society was founded in 1934 as the Group for Historical Research on Wilkinsburg Village and Environs, 1788-1887. The purpose of the Society today is to promote interest in the history and landmarks of the Borough of Wilkinsburg and to collect, preserve, and publish historical data and documents.

You are encouraged to assist in our purpose by contributing photographs and written information to the Wilkinsburg Historical Society c/o Wilkinsburg Public Library, 605 Ross Avenue, Wilkinsburg, PA 15221.

Wilkinsburg High School

Just as firm as a mountain, these years you have stood,
Like a free running fountain of knowledge so good,
Just as straight as an arrow you've pointed the way
And directed our lives just a little each day.

You have housed many sorrows, you've known of our joys,
You have steadied our thoughts by your unswerving poise,
You have grown into our love, made your way into our heart,
And from there, dear old building, you'll never depart.

Wm. H. Merrifield, '24

You're only a cold stone building
To the casual passer-by,
But to us who've worked and played in you
You mean a lot, old High.

You mean the knowledge of lessons learned;
The spirit of things well done;
Of games hard fought and games well played;
And days of hearty fun.

You've sheltered our dearest friendships;
You've helped us to dare and do;
And we cherish the high ideals
You gave us, Red and Blue.

So whatever we are in the future,
Whatever we may do,
We shall look back down the years, dear High
In gratitude to you.

Ruth Fiske, '27

Chapter 1 - The Early Years, 1840-1910

The History of Our Schools:
Oration delivered by senior student Joe Marcy
at Commencement Exercises at Graham Field, Thursday, June 3, 1937

About the year 1840 Mr. James Kelly, a prominent citizen of the town, for this district at that time was Wilkins Township, contributed money toward the first public school in this district.

It was a simple log structure with one room, located somewhere near the site of the present Semple School. The next building in the district was a one-story brick building situated on what is now the corner of Center and Wallace Avenues. It was later used as a carpenter shop where most of the caskets for this district were made. This was followed in 1850 by a two-room brick structure on the same site but nearer North Avenue. In 1872 a frame building was built on the same site but facing on Wallace Avenue. These buildings were all public schools, but in 1852 a private Academy was erected on the southwest corner of Center and Wallace. This building was bought in 1875 to provide more room for the growing school.

Until 1877 the village school system had been rather complicated. At that time, Mr. John D. Anderson, who was interested in education and the schools of the community, was selected principal and given charge of the schools. From that time, the schools of Wilkinsburg took great strides forward until they were considered among the best in Allegheny County. This fact was proved by the great number of students from outlying districts who preferred coming to school in Wilkinsburg under Mr. Anderson's supervision, to attending the schools in their own district. At that time, the primary grades were taught in the new frame building which contained four school rooms and a hall where town meetings were held. The intermediate grades were housed in the old brick building next door. The grammar grades were housed in the old academy across the street. Assisting Mr. Anderson were five teachers.

In 1882 the community was so pleased with its school system that it erected a fifteen-room, three-story brick building on the site of the present Junior High School. It was built at a cost of $36,200. On the completion of this building, the older ones were sold.

1856-1861 Wilkinsburg Academy
Wallace Avenue at Center Street

1882 -1890 Wilkinsburg Public School
Wallace Avenue between Center Street and Mill Street

On March 19, 1883, fire broke out in the director's room of the new building and destroyed all books, minutes, records and former school history. It is for this reason that we have today no definite records of our early school history. Wilkins Township became the independent borough of Wilkinsburg in 1887 and Mr. John D. Anderson, being principal of the schools, was put in charge of the public schools of Wilkinsburg. It was in this year that the first class of three girls graduated from Wilkinsburg.

John D. Anderson

1887 graduating class
Emily Munson
Alice Potter
Clarissa Moffitt

First Ward School (later named Horner) 1890-1916

On January 13, 1890, the Horner School caught fire and burned to the ground. The pupils were housed in the various churches for schooling. At this time it was decided to erect two buildings, one of 15 rooms to replace the one burned and another for those students in the Third Ward.

After the fire of 1890, the Board met at the house of the president, Mr. J. S. Stevenson who moved that two schools be built: one (McNair) in the Second Ward corner of Center and South, of 15 to 16 rooms, and another (Kelly) in the Third Ward. Kelly School was built in 1890 as a two-story building on the corner of Pitt and McNair Streets. Later, a third floor was added to house the high school program.

KELLY SCHOOL

1890-1969 (torn down 1969)

The school board awarded a contract to build a school building in the Second Ward at a cost of $38,500. This new building was located on the corner of Center and South Avenues, and later named McNair School.

McNair School
1895-1950

The idea of a commencement was first introduced by the class of 1893. Lacking an auditorium, the graduating class gave a short program and received its diplomas in the Odd Fellows' Hall on Penn Avenue. In 1897 a complete course of academic subjects which included Latin, Geometry, Physics, History, English and Rhetoric, was added to the curriculum.

Odd Fellows' Hall at 727 Penn Avenue

Mr. E. J. Shives, who had been principal of the public schools, was elected superintendent. Because of the crowded condition in the schools, the Board of Education thought it best to erect another building in the First Ward; therefore, on September 23, 1902, contracts were let for Semple School. It is interesting to note that until 1903, the three buildings already erected and the one about to be erected had no names and were referred to merely by the ward in which they were located. Since this system was awkward and difficult, the buildings were given names that we know today - Horner, McNair, Kelly and Semple. All were named for prominent citizens of the community.

SEMPLE SCHOOL

Swissvale Avenue at Laketon Road
1903-1974, later torn down

The period from 1900 until 1911 was one of rapid growth, not only in the number of students but also in the variety and size of the curriculum. A few years before, most of the academic subjects had been added. In 1901 physical training and drawing had been adopted. During these eleven years the student enrollment increased from 1300 to nearly 3000 and number of teachers and principals from 45 to 72. The class of 1900 consisting of nine girls was the first to complete the three year course in the high school department. The class of 1907 was the first to complete the present four year schedule.

Class of 1900

Because of the overcrowded conditions at this time, the Board of Directors let contracts for Johnston School in 1906, and for the high school building in 1911. Previous to this time, the high school had been housed in three rooms in the McNair building and later in the entire third floor of the Kelly School.

Johnston School, built in 1906 had a major fire in 1920 which destroyed the top story. The school was rebuilt adding two floors in 1922. The school is located at 1256 Franklin Avenue.

For the first time, the students of the high school department had a building all to themselves in which they could take the courses and have the entertainment and enjoyment that they wanted. Previously there had been no gymnasium, no science rooms, no library, nor study halls; the new building was equipped with all these. The students were quick to make use of these necessities, and in those years started many of the entertainments and social activities that we have today, such as the Gym Exhibit, the Junior and Senior Proms, and many of the clubs. Under Mr. William C. Graham's supervision athletics made great progress. In 1903 he organized Wilkinsburg's first varsity football and in 1906 a paid coach was hired. Our first W.P.I.A.L. championships in football were won in 1914, 1915, and 1916. In appreciation of Mr. Graham's work, the new athletic field, dedicated in 1916, was named for him.

JUNIOR HIGH SCHOOL

1918-1985, sold in 1990
Horner Junior High, now Hosanna House
Wallace Avenue between Center Street and Mill Street

For the second time the Horner School building burned to the ground, and the present Junior High School replaced it in 1918. The Johnston School was also destroyed by fire and rebuilt in 1922. Allison School was then built so that the lower grades might be separated from the congested Junior High School. Turner School was then built for the convenience of the students who live in that area. During the next few years the lack of adequate health facilities was felt in the school system, and for that reason the Open Air School in the McNair building was opened; this was followed by an Opportunity School for retarded pupils. In 1922 a dental clinic was started in the Junior High School. The work of this clinic was done by the Senior Class of the Dental School at the University of Pittsburgh. The same year school banking was introduced in the schools, and has in every way proved to be a success.

Allison School, 1927-1985, sold in 1993
Wallace Avenue at Mill Street

Once more, as before the building of the high school, the same complication of over-crowded rooms and classes seemed to be arising. The situation soon became so serious that the two corridors along the auditorium balcony were enclosed and turned into study halls. It was necessary to suspend chapel in order to use the auditorium for a study hall, and the mechanical drawing classes were forced to lower the curtain and meet back-stage. The school also installed lockers in the halls for those who were without cloakroom facilities.

Turner School, 1927 to present
1833 Laketon Road

Wilkinsburg High School was built in 1910-1911 and dedicated March 30, 1911.

Finally when it became impossible to accommodate the increasing number of students, the School Board added the new addition in 1929 to the High School. The new addition, including the boys' gymnasium and the auditorium, has improved conditions temporarily, but even today it is almost impossible to seat the whole student body in chapel.

This has been the story of the rapid growth of our schools. We are indeed indebted to Mr. Anderson, Mr. Martin, Mr. Allison, Mr. Graham, and the school boards who have served so faithfully, and to the many other men and women who have served their community by serving their school. *End of oration by Joe Marcy*

Installed when the school was built in 1911, two bronze plaques flank the Wallace Avenue entrance to Wilkinsburg High School. These bronze markers are visible in many of the class pictures taken on the front steps.

William C. Graham comes to Wilkinsburg

In 1903, Mr. W.C. Graham was elected principal of the high school. William C. Graham, educator, civic leader, WHS Principal and Superintendent of Wilkinsburg Schools, was both academically and athletically minded. All of his life he was a huge booster of WHS sports activities, teams, and groups. William Graham also conducted chapel exercises at WHS each morning for many years, read Scripture, made announcements and always encouraged students in their classes and the school's sports programs. Beloved "Willie" Graham served as WHS Principal from 1903 to December, 1928, and as Superintendent from January, 1929 to 1941.

In 1903 Professor Graham encouraged and started a football team. High school in those days was the third floor of the Kelly Elementary School in the Third Ward. The boys who enrolled for the athletic program purchased their own football, furnished their own playing clothes and formed the WHS Athletic Association. They played on the grounds at Braddock Avenue at Forbes Avenue and used McMurray's

William C. Graham

Laundry nearby as their dressing room. Student high school tuition in 1904 was $50 per year. An outstanding administrator, his achievement is unique in local school history. During his service, the thousands of young men and women who graduated from WHS have earned for it a scholastic rating that was virtually unsurpassed. The school, during his administration, achieved a remarkable reputation for a modern and finely equipped plant, for its progressive organization, for its excellent athletic program, and for its distinctive high school chapel service - all of which crowned its unusually high academic ranking. As a WHS football fan, he often wore boots and a raincoat and "played out" each play on the field, chasing up and down the sidelines. A great family man, he was a church leader in the Second United Presbyterian Church and for decades was Wilkinsburg's best known individual. The Graham family resided for many years on the Penn Avenue hill just above Graham Field.

1907 football squad
Some of the students created their own "W" to sew on their jersey as a sign of pride in their Wilkinsburg team.

Spoon Tradition from the Senior Class began in 1901.

The first presentation of the traditional spoon was in 1901. At commencement, the senior class officers would present the 6 foot long wooden spoon to the junior class officers. The spoon symbolized the responsibility for upholding the school ideals of loyalty, honor, leadership and scholarship.

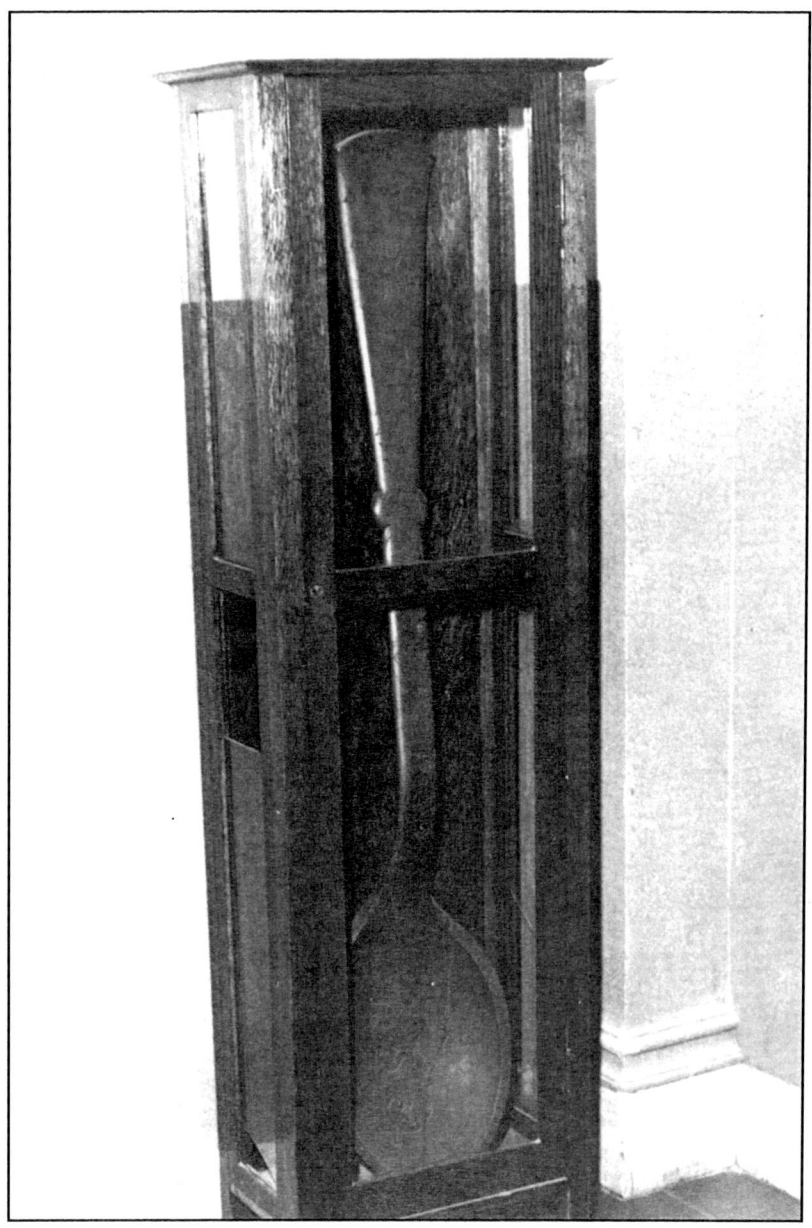

Symbolic wooden spoon since 1901

During presentation the seniors would state: "To aid you in your efforts, to give you an inspiration and a reminder of the great class before you, we present you this scepter of power, this symbol of peace, this power of learning."

The spoon was safely kept in this glass case in the school library. The tradition continued for over 75 years.

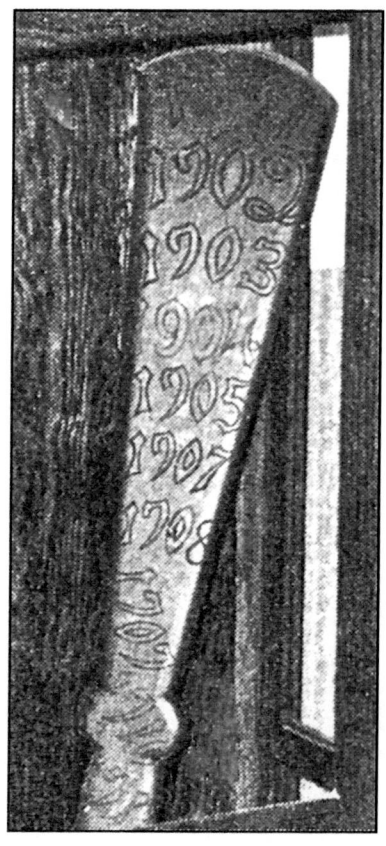

Dates were carved in the handle of the spoon for the first eleven years that it was presented, beginning in 1901.

This is the 1905 graduating class in Wilkinsburg. At that time high school classes were still held in Kelly and McNair Schools.

"Review" Editorial Staff 1907-8

These high school students served as the 1907-08 staff of the "Review", the school newspaper which was written and published six times per school year.

The 1906-1907 WHS baseball team played their games at the Braddock Avenue field which was located near Forbes Avenue.

1905 Wilkinsburg High School baseball team breeds a future Hall of Famer

One prominent player who later became famous in baseballs' major league is William "Bill" McKechnie. Bill McKechnie (1886-1965) attended Wilkinsburg Schools and later began his professional career in 1907 with the Pittsburgh Pirates. He became the Pirates' manager in 1922. Under his management, they won the 1925 World Series. The St. Louis Cardinals won the National League pennant under his management in 1928. McKechnie also managed the Cincinnati Reds, winning the National League pennant in 1939, and the World Series in 1940. He was elected to the National Baseball Hall of Fame in 1962.

Geider   Cratty   Dipple   Fleeger   Beam   Orton

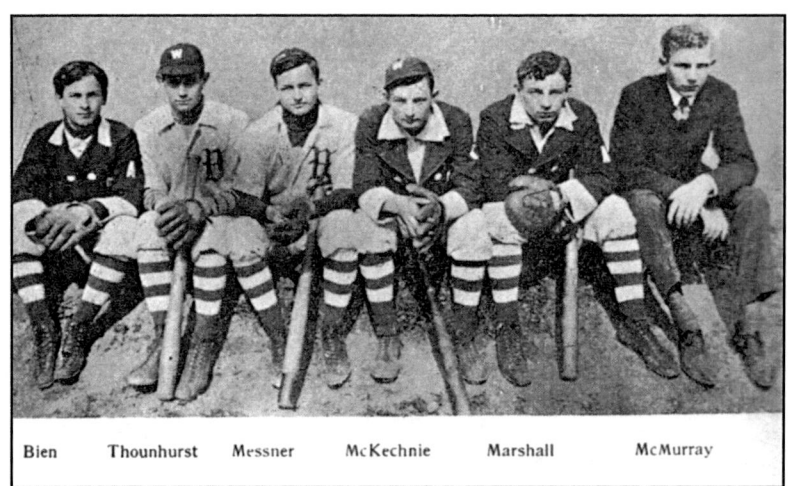

Bien   Thounhurst   Messner   McKechnie   Marshall   McMurray

1905 Wilkinsburg High baseball team

1907 Bill McKechnie as a Pirate

1912 at Forbes Field

1925 as Pirate manager

1962 National Baseball Hall of Fame

Wilkinsburg High boy's hockey team defeated East Liberty Academy in a championship Interscholastic Hockey League game at the Duquesne Garden on December 21, 1905. Two weeks later on January 7, 1906, the Pittsburgh Gazette reported that "the race in the Triple Amateur Hockey league has settled itself for the present by Wilkinsburg winning from Knoxville Kountry Klub. This prevents any other team to tie with Wilkinsburg for first place. All the teams are now playing fast hockey, but Wilkinsburg's fast forward line has kept it in the lead."

In 1907-1908 Wilkinsburg High had a great baseball team. The "H" on their uniforms distinguished the High School team from local semi-pro and amateur teams. These boys played at DC and AC Park. The full name of the park was Duquesne Country and Athletic Club Park, located in the Hay-North-Pitt-Hill block in Wilkinsburg.

1909-1910 was the first year for track at Wilkinsburg High School. In the early years football, baseball and track events were usually held at DC and AC Park on Hay Street and North Avenue.

1 Edna Reitz, 2 Clarence W. Hagan, 3 Cora Gerwig, 4 Jean Donaldson, 5 Reuben Henning, 6 Annie Luther, 7 Hiram C. Davis, 8 John Lutz, 9 Ruth Downing, 10 A. Clyde Young, 11 C. Leo Weinman, 12 Edna Fisher, 13 W. Lyle McDaniel, 14 Stanley Siemon, 15 Marie Munroe.

In 1908 the graduating class included thirteen girls and seventeen boys. Also noteworthy is the graduation of the first African-American student from Wilkinsburg High School, James Miles.

16 Eugenie Senn, 17 Charles Raisig, 18 Henrietta Reinhart, 19 John Newell, 20 Roy Hodgdon, 21 Mary McCance, 22 George Ratcliffe, 23 Zellers Luther, 24 Leah Burkhart, 25 William T. Lytle, 26 A. Jay Bien, 27 Dunning Hart Ross, 28 Anne Doherty, 29 Florence Keys, 30 James Miles.

Chapter 2 - High School Building and Dedication, 1911

Dedication Address - March 30, 1911   by J.G. Sansom, President of School Board

The committee on dedication that arranged the excellent program for this evening assigned to me a fifteen-minute address to give a history of the schools of Wilkinsburg, and the building of the High School Building. I will ask your indulgence by giving this briefly in reading from the manuscript thus prepared.

It is a great pleasure to present to you one who is the leader in high schools of Western Pennsylvania, Director of the Pittsburgh High School, Prof. Edward Rynearson.

We are most fortunate to have with us this evening a former resident of Wilkinsburg, one who has served on the School Board, also as secretary of the board for a number of years. This one had much to do with our school's progress - Rev. John A. Burnett of Monmouth, Illinois.

A familiar person to many in the audience, the leading advocate of grade schools and a most efficient Superintendent of Allegheny County Schools - Dr. Samuel Hamilton.

For the main cause of this meeting, the dedication of the High School Building, we are greatly favored by having the dedicatory address by a learned educator of this country - Dr. Nathan C. Schaeffer, State Superintendent of Public Instruction.

The first school house in the village of Wilkinsburg, of which I have any record, was located between Coal and Swissvale Streets, north of Penn Avenue. It was a one-room frame structure and was later displaced by a two-room brick building on Center Street, between Wallace and North Avenues. About the time Wilkinsburg was annexed to the City of Pittsburgh as the 37th ward, an additional building was erected at the corner of Wallace Avenue and Center Street, directly across Wallace Avenue from the home of Mr. William Turner.

This was a frame structure of two rooms and a tar paper roof, a building which would send thrills of joy up and down the spinal columns of the present-day advocates of the "open air" treatment. It was other thrills that permeated the system of the principal after each heavy fall of snow when he had to climb a ladder with a shovel and free the roof of snow to avoid giving the pupils a shower bath when the heat of the rooms combined with rays of the sun caused the snow to melt.

Directly across Center Street stood a building consisting of four small rooms and one large room, used as an academy, the small rooms furnishing a residence for the principal of the academy. As the academy had recently been discontinued the School Board got the use of this building and opened at first two - and later three- of these rooms for public school use.

At this time Wilkinsburg, Edgewood, Brushton and the Crescent districts in Pittsburgh were all one sub-district of Wilkins township, and as such had been annexed to Pittsburgh. After somewhat protracted litigation the district ceased to be a part of Pittsburgh and was erected into a new district known as Sterrett township, in honor of the judge who made the decree in the local courts and who afterward became a member of the Supreme Court of this State.

Shortly after separation from Pittsburgh the school facilities were wholly inadequate and the board prepared to meet the demand for more room. A large lot about 200x264 feet, bounded by Wallace and North Avenues and Mill Street, was purchased and a three-story brick building erected containing 15 school rooms, 2 offices and an auditorium capable of seating about 400 persons.

By many well-meaning persons, and others, the board was severely censured for extravagance in erecting a building which would not be filled for 50 years and having a hall which would never be filled - so they said - all of which shows that the use of the hammer is not a lost art.

This building was destroyed by fire in 1890 and the schools were scattered into vacant halls and churches until the present structure known as the Horner school, was erected on the site of the burnt schoolhouse. This was almost immediately followed by an 8-room building in the Third ward, which was soon filled, thus compelling the board to provide more room. This crowded condition was temporarily relieved by the erection of a school house in the Second ward - the McNair.

Needing more room, the two-story 8 room building in the Third ward was changed into the large three-story building and the newly organized High School found its first home in this building. The rapid growth in school population soon compelled the erection of two more buildings - the Semple in the First ward and the Johnston in the Second ward.

The High School, having seen the rapid growth of the grade schools, concluded it would do some growing on its own account. As it was a lusty, vigorous youth it soon outgrew its home, took up quarters in the two Second ward schools; it was being cared for in three different buildings. As those rooms will be needed to accommodate the rapidly growing grade schools, a separate building for high school became imperative.

As a result of the rapid growth of both the grade school and the High School population, the present building in which we meet tonight was projected, and after many annoying but unavoidable delays has at last been completed.

We shall not trespass on your time and patience by a recital of its history from the inception to the completion of the structure; but we would be guilty of the basest ingratitude did we not embrace the present opportunity of expressing our hearty appreciation of the loyal support and encouragement given to the School Board by the citizens, who permitted us, by a popular vote, to construct a building which is an honor to our town; a building which is unsurpassed by any other of its kind in Western Pennsylvania; a building which will meet the demands of the community for many years to come.

Wilkinsburg High School was built in 1910-1911 by the C. H. Kerr Company.
The architect was Thomas H. Scott. The building was dedicated on March 30, 1911.

Cost and Construction of Wilkinsburg High School in 1911

Continuation of Dedication Address by J. G. Sansom, President of the School Board

Cost - As to its cost, I would say, briefly, that including the grounds, furniture and equipment complete, also the concrete walks, the total cost is $368,000.

Construction - As to its construction, you can see that while the school room floors, doors and desks are of wood, the building is comparatively fire proof. The outside walls are stone and brick, while the interior walls are of hollow tile. The corridor is tile, while the stairways are of iron and marble. The roof is tile, flashings, water ducts and spouting of copper.

While the building is practically fireproof, additional precautions to secure the absolute safety of the students will be found in the five exits, together with two separate systems of stairways, one in the front and one in the rear of the building, each extending from basement to top of the structure.

Wilkinsburg High School's New Home Under Erection

Division - The building consists of sub-basement, basement, first floor, second floor, third floor.

Sub-Basement - In the sub-basement are located the Gymnasium, Locker rooms and Shower Baths. These lockers have closed fronts. Each boy or girl using the lockers is provided with a private key which secures the safety of any articles in the locker.

Basement - In the Basement proper are located the Running Track, Manual Training Department, Janitor's room, Supply room, fresh air and foul air rooms, waste-paper room which receives all waste paper from a chute connecting with each floor.

Here are also located the fans connected with the heating and ventilating system: one supplying fresh air to the various rooms and the other taking out the foul air. Here is also found the air washer. A plan by which the fresh air is passed through a fine spray of water which washes all impurities from the air and after drying it sends it to the several rooms as near absolute purity as any mechanical device is presently able to produce.

If this does not kill the germs in the air it will, we hope, wash them so that they enter the rooms with clean hands and feet. Also, as cleanliness is next to Godliness, we may claim this device is a means of grace.

Class Room W. H. S.

First Floor - The first floor contains seven large school rooms and seven large cloak rooms. A general and a private office for the Superintendent and for the Principal, director's room, teacher's room, supply room local telephone exchange for use in the building. On this floor are two fireproof vaults for the storing of papers, records, etc. A unique feature of our cloak room is found in the fact that entrance to them can be gained only from the school room; they open into the corridor but cannot be entered from the corridor. This arrangement is a safeguard of the contents of pockets against the "get-rich-quick" fellow who may be prowling in the corridor.

The Auditorium and dressing rooms for same are located on this floor, flanked on either side by large doors opening into North Avenue, and opening also into a corridor leading to the main entrance on Wallace Avenue. The seating capacity, including balcony, is about 1,100 persons. As you can readily see, there is no use for a further description.

High School Auditorium, where the Dedication Exercises Were Held

Second Floor - The second floor contains seven large school rooms and seven large cloak rooms. A library containing the various reference books used by the students and teachers; a reading room, a teacher's room and a reception room. The reading room and the reception room may be converted into class rooms if future needs require it.

Reading Room

Literary Society Hall

Chemistry Laboratory

Third Floor This floor contains one class room, one lecture hall, which may be changed into two class rooms by means of a rolling partition now in place; five cloak rooms, one recitation room, one banking room, one type-writing room, the necessary rooms for commercial studies, one sewing room, one science hall, two storage rooms, physical and chemical laboratories, drawing room and a dark room for science work.

Typewriting Room—Commercial Department

For social occasions with a view to use as a domestic science department there are a kitchen, dining room and banquet hall on the third floor. At present the kitchen only has been furnished. As the domestic science department is located on the top floor we can assure our friends of high-class work by high-class students.

The time shown by the clocks in each room is governed by a master clock on the first floor, which is run by electricity.

The rooms are cleaned by a vacuum cleaning system operated by a motor in the basement. All dirt from the rooms is carried to a receptacle in the basement, a burying ground for germs of high and low degree.

There are other features to which we could draw your attention, but as they are of minor importance we shall not trespass on your time further than to add in closing that Wilkinsburg deserved a High School Building, modern and complete in all its appointments and the Board of Directors have faithfully tried to furnish it. *End of Dedication Address by J.G.Sansom*

Physics Laboratory

Science Hall

The new WHS Gymnasium was the setting for the Junior Prom. In the 1911 "Review" is a description of the event. "The Junior Prom, which was held Friday evening, May 19th, in our new school, went down in school history as the finest affair of its kind ever held. This being the most important social event of the year, great attention was given to every detail, the music, decorations, etc., being very pleasing. The delightful program, the dancing and the delicious refreshments, all helped to make this the most enjoyable reception ever held in WHS. The Seniors, who were the guests of honor, were royally entertained and departed with congratulations and best wishes of the Juniors, who will take their place in school-life next year."

W. H. S. Gymnasium, Where the Junior Prom Was Held.

The Senior Promenade is one of the most important social functions of the school year. The custom of holding Senior Proms originated in WHS when Superintendent Shives, at the turn of the century, gave a banquet for the graduating class and the faculty in the Hotel Chatham. The next year the senior girls gave a party for the senior class at Dr. Parry's home. Parties at private homes were continued until 1905. In 1905 a senior dance was held at the Pennwood Club on Ross Avenue where annual dances were held until 1911. In 1911 the high school was built and the juniors gave the seniors a Prom in the gymnasium. The juniors continued to give dances for the seniors until 1915. When the evangelist Billy Sunday had his tabernacle here in Wilkinsburg in 1915, a number of students of the high school and a few citizens of the borough, influenced by his preaching, asked that the School Board prohibit dancing in the schools. The School Board approved this plan, and until 1930 no dances of any kind were allowed in the school buildings. In 1930 a committee took a petition from the student body to the School Board asking for the privilege of again holding dances in the school. Permission was granted by the board and the Senior Prom was held in the new gymnasium under the charge of a committee of senior A's and B's with the president of Senior A class acting as chairman. We hope that our proms have come to stay permanently, because they are well on the way toward establishing another cherished tradition of our school. *Information from the 1931 Annual*

Wilkinsburg High School's History by Professor W.T. Slater
Presented during Wilkinsburg High School's dedication, March 30, 1911

When Did Our High School Begin?

Now that we occupy a building suited to our growing need and specially equipped for high school work, it may not be amiss to look back a moment and attempt to answer a question asked by students: "When did the Wilkinsburg High School Begin?"

I. Course of Study

Some High School work was done in the Wilkinsburg public schools twenty-eight years ago. A Teachers' Monthly Report book exists, the only one saved from the fire, in which the books named as texts in the highest grade are the following: Robinson's Higher Arithmetic, Brooks' Normal Mental Arithmetic, Brooks' Algebra, Warren's Physical Geography, Hart's Rhetoric, Steele's Natural Philosophy, Forbriger's Drawing, Burt's English Grammar. This report is for 1884.

Professor W. T. Slater

In 1885 the only change noted is the use of Cooley's instead of Steele's Natural Philosophy, Civil Government was soon added; and in almost every year after 1886 a class in book-keeping completed six or eight sets of double-entry, together with the usual auxiliary books. Sometimes there was a class in Plane Geometry. So many students were preparing for teachers examinations that a class in Theory of Teaching was contented to recite to the Principal after four o'clock, the usual time for dismissal. The subjects taught in the High School Class varied somewhat from year to year as the school became more crowded or the class was younger. In 1896 there was a class in General History.

In 1897 the Board of Education added more than a full year of academic subjects and employed Mr. A. Bert Allison to have charge of the work. By this arrangement pupils were offered Latin, Geometry, Physics, General History, English Literature and Rhetoric, in combination with high school subjects already taught in that department. Mr. Allison also had a student or two in Greek. In 1898 English History was added. About 1901, the course of study was extended to give three years' work; and since 1906 no student has been graduated with less than four years' work.

II. Diplomas

The Allegheny County Teachers' Association in 1875 prepared a diploma to be issued to pupils outside Pittsburgh or Allegheny who should pass a satisfactory examination. The examinations were conducted by a committee from the Association. Wilkinsburg pupils secured these diplomas from the first, but steadily refused to call the examinations difficult.

The Wilkinsburg Board of Education, in 1890, first issued its own diploma to pupils who had completed its course of study and passed the principal's examinations. The passing mark was now 80 per cent. The diploma was headed: "Wilkinsburg Public Schools, High School Department," and declared the person named "a graduate of this institution and entitled to this diploma."

III. Commencements

The Class of 1893 gave a short program at the close of the term, in Odd Fellows' Hall. At its conclusion the President of the Board addressed the class and presented the diplomas. Thereafter, public exercises were given by the graduating class annually, and were popularly known as the "High School Commencement." It gave students something definite to which they looked forward, and it never failed to pack the largest hall or church.

The reader is by this time able to answer for himself the question in our heading. Our present four years' course has been a gradual development. We have come up to the present conditions through all the grades of high school now recognized by the State Department of Pennsylvania. Before the State Department recognized any sort of high school, we had a good one-year course under the direct management of the Principal of Schools.

The Homes of the High School

At the time of "the fire", the High School Class had its quarters on the first floor of the beautiful three-story structure that occupied the site of the present Horner building. When the High School and last grammar grade classes reassembled after the fire, it was in the old United Brethren Church on Ross Avenue, beyond Coal Street. One winter followed in the old Methodist Episcopal Church on Wallace Avenue; and then the Class of '93 was sent to the former Third Ward School. The classes of 1894 and 1895 were lodged in room 15 of the Horner School. Rapid school expansion crowded the High School and advanced grammar classes out again, and for most of one year they were housed in the Lohr building on South Avenue and Wood Street, moving from these halls to the McNair School as soon as it was completed. Only teachers who have spent a series of years trying to do without school desks and equipment while they waited for carpenters to finish new buildings can understand what such a change meant. In this building the enlarged and reorganized High School began; and in this place it continued to be until the remodeled and enlarged Kelly School furnished better accommodations in its light and airy third floor.

At first, five rooms of our "flat" were sufficient, number nineteen being occupied by the advanced Grammar grade of that school; but after one year all the rooms were required, and an overflow section invaded the Principal's office. This beginning was followed by constant High School encroachment upon second floor space, until this year, when four second-story rooms were used by High School classes. This, however, is only part of our expansion. In 1907 the First Year class, consisting of four rooms, was placed in McNair School. The year following, Johnston School having been completed, the new first year class was divided, two rooms being sent to Johnston School and two retained at McNair School. This plan was continued until April first.

The High School teachers have for years felt sincere regret that so many Primary and Grammar grade pupils have suffered some discomfort on our account. Many have had to go to some other ward than their own because of crowded conditions growing out of the need of a High School building. In going to our new home we congratulate them that they will be able to return to theirs.

End of Wilkinsburg High School's History by W. T. Slater

Class of 1895

Lohr Building, corner of South and Wood where classes were held in the mid 1890s.

In 1911 a complete college preparatory education became available in the new High School.

The Faculty

W. C. GRAHAM.....................Principal

HELEN H. FARIS................Head German

ESTHER M. SMITH..........Assistant German

JANET M. LAMBIE.....................Latin

J. H. EDGERTON.......................Latin

S. M. KANAGY..........Latin and Mathematics

CHESTER B. STORY.............Head English

CLARA H. WILKINS...........French-English

V. E. KNAPPENBERGER......Assistant English

L. O. PACKER...............Head Mathematics

A. E. RICKSECKER...............Head Science

WM. T. SLATER.................Head History

INDIA STEPHENSON....Assistant Mathematics

T. D. BROWN, JR...History and Director Athletics

JOHN E. FANCHER..........Head Commercial

H. E. ROBINSON.............Assistant Science

BERTHA B. CLEMENT.................Music

Z. CORINNE BLAKESLEE............Drawing

Course of Study

FIRST YEAR.

ACADEMIC. Required.	COMMERCIAL. Required.
English Composition, 3.	English Composition, 3.
Classics, 2.	Classics, 2.
Latin, 5.	Commercial Arithmetic, 5.
Algebra, 5.	Algebra, 5.
Physical Geography, 3.	Commercial Geography, 3.
Civics, 2.	Civics, 2.

SECOND YEAR.

Required.	Required.
Rhetoric, 3.	Rhetoric, 3.
Classics, 2.	Classics, 2.
Algebra, 5.	Algebra, 5.
Ancient History, 5.	Ancient History, 5.
Elective.	Orthography, 5.
Select 1, may take both.	Penmanship, 5.
Caesar with Composition, 5.	
German, 5.	

THIRD YEAR.

Required.	Required.
English Literature, 3.	English Literature, 3.
Classics 2.	Classics, 2.
Plane Geometry, 5.	Correspondence, 2.
Elective.	Elective.
Select 2, may take 3.	Select Three.
Cicero with Composition, 5.	Bookkeeping, 5.
German, 5.	Stenography with Typewriting, 10.
French, 5.	German, 5.
Physics, 6.	French, 5.
Botany, 5.	Physics, 6.
Mediaeval and Modern History, 5.	Botany, 5.
	Mediaeval and Modern History, 5.

FOURTH YEAR.

Required.	Required.
American Literature, 3.	American Literature, 3.
Classics, 2.	Classics, 2.
Elective.	Elective.
Select 3, may take 4.	Select 3,
Virgil, 5.	Second year Bookkeeping, with Business Practice, 5.
German, 5.	
Greek, 5.	Second year Stenography with Typewriting, 10.
French, 5.	
Solid Geometry, 2½.	Commercial Law, 3.
Plane Trigometry, 2½.	German, 5.
Advanced Algebra, 2½.	French, 5.
Physics, 6.	Physics, 6.
Botany, 5.	Botany, 5.
Chemistry, 5.	American History and Civics, 5.
American History and Civics, 5.	

Provision is made for those desiring to teach whereby they may elect a review of the common branches during their senior year.

Pupils may complete the Commercial branches in two years. Those pursuing this plan can be given a certificate showing the work done in the school.

In 1907, a crisis was reached in our high school system. The school had grown from a single class to four separate classes, which, due to crowded conditions, were divided among the schools of the borough. The Board of Directors realized that success could not be gained by division of classes which destroyed the unity of the school. The only relief the Board could see was the construction of a high school building large enough to house all classes and to supply members of each class with a thorough college preparatory education. Students canvassed every house in the borough, urging the citizens to vote for the bond issue, to which many citizens objected, saying that the proposed building was too large and that it would not be filled in twenty years. But, despite objections, the building was approved, and in the spring of 1911 the school was ready for occupancy. The faculty list and course of study for 1911 was printed in the school publication, the Review.

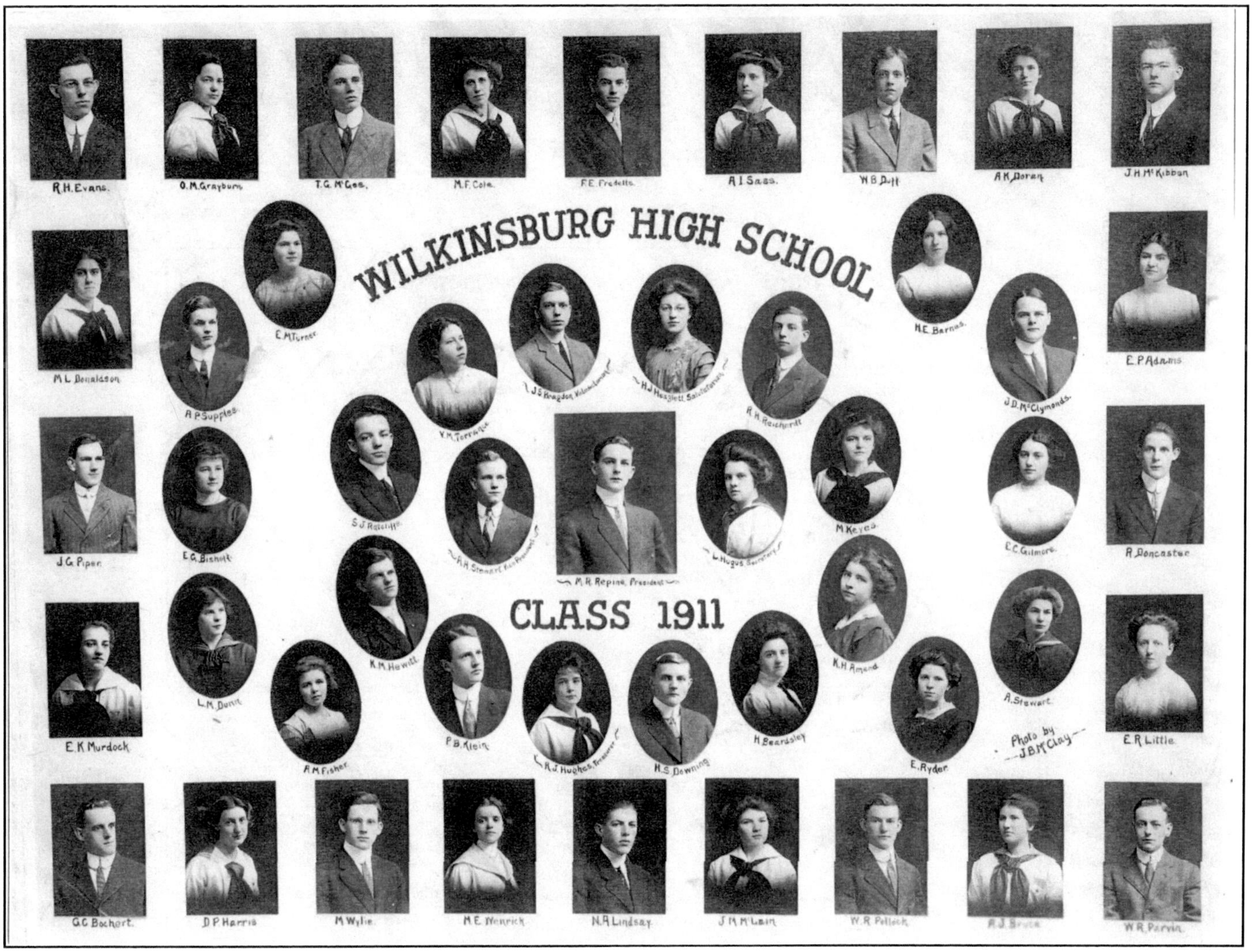

CLASS OF 1911

WILKINSBURG HIGH SCHOOL

Commencement Exercises

IN THE HIGH SCHOOL AUDITORIUM
MAY 25, 8 O'CLOCK

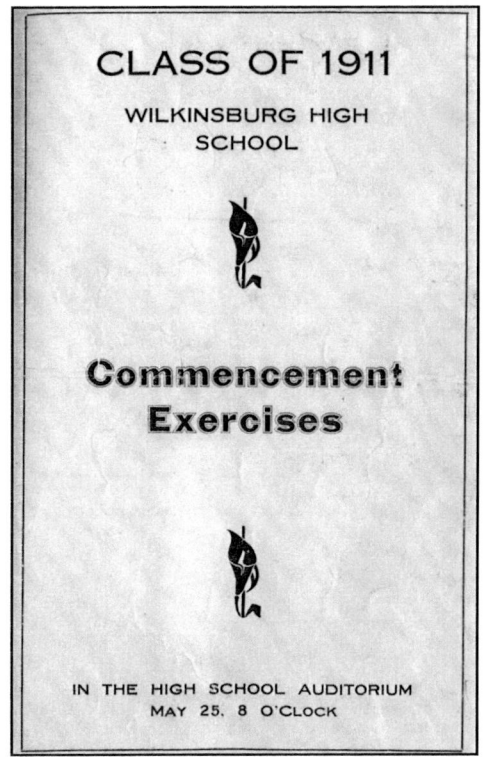

The class of 1911 was the first to graduate from the beautiful new Wilkinsburg High School.

There were 49 students in the senior class, 22 boys and 27 girls.

The Board of Directors issued an informative 29 page manual.

ANNUAL REPORT OF WILKINSBURG SCHOOLS, 1910-1911.

Whole number of schools...	
Average number of months taught............................	9
Number of male teachers employed............................	10
Number of female teachers employed.........................	66
Average salaries of males per month.........................$	148.70
Average salaries of females per month.......................	88.58
Number of male pupils attending all the schools in the district..	1,525
Number of female pupils attending all the schools in the district	1,552
Whole number of pupils in attendance........................	3 077
Average daily attendance of pupils in the district..............	2,520
Average percentage of attendance............................	96
Cost of each pupil per month................................$	3.28
Number of mills levied for school purposes..................	5 10-12
Number of mills levied for building purposes.................	1 8-12
Amount in dollars levied for school purposes................	116,873.02
Amount in dollars levied for building purposes..............	33,392.28
Total amount levied, including $1.00 per capita tax.........$	150,265.30

SESSIONS.

The session of school for the First, Second and Third Grades is from nine o'clock to eleven in the morning and from one to three in the afternoon.

The session for all grades above the Third is from nine o'clock to eleven-thirty in the morning and from 1 to three-thirty in the afternoon.

The session of the High School is from eight-thirty to eleven-forty in the morning and from one ten to three twenty-five o'clock in the afternoon.

EXAMINATIONS.

First examination, January 15, 17 and 18; Second examination, May 27, 28 and 29.

GRADE NECESSARY FOR PROMOTION.

The grade necessary for promotion is a general average of 75 per cent. with no branch with an average below 70 per cent.

Pupils who have been two years in one grade may be promoted at the discretion of the principal at the beginning of the third year, if the test warrants such promotion.

PROMOTIONS.

All promotions will be made at the first and middle of each term. Pupils who are found to be in advance of their classes or behind their classes may be replaced at any time by the principal.

16

REQUIREMENTS FOR ENTRANCE TO THE HIGH SCHOOL.

All pupils desiring to enter the High School shall be required to take an examination conducted by the Teachers of the Eighth Grade and the Principals and Superintendent, unless certificates from other High Schools may be deemed by the faculty sufficient guarantee of scholarship.

The examination for Eighth Grade pupils desiring to enter the High School will be held during the second week in Jan. and the last week in May.

RATES OF TUITION FOR NON-RESIDENTS.

Pupils who reside outside of the district and attend school in Wilkinsburg will be required to pay tuition as follows: High School, $60.00 per term; Grades $27.00 per term; and all to be paid in advance. No pupil to be admitted unless a receipt for payment of tuition is presented to the principal, or satisfactory arrangements have been made.

ANNUAL TEACHERS' EXAMINATION.

The annual teachers' examination will be held in the office of the superintendent June 6 and 7, beginning at 8 o'clock a. m.

GRADE MEETINGS.

The teachers of each grade will be called together frequently for conferences. The Principals will hold frequent meetings of the Teachers under their charge.

PRINCIPALS' MEETINGS.

A meeting of the principals will be held on the Second and Fourth Monday evenings of each school month, at four o'clock, in the superintendent's office.

17

TWO YEAR COMMERCIAL COURSE.

FIRST YEAR	SECOND YEAR
REQUIRED	**REQUIRED**
Commercial English (3)	Correspondence (3)
English Classics (2)	English Classics (2)
Commercial Arithmetic (5)	
Penmanship with Orthography (5)	**ELECTIVE**
	Bookkeeping with Business
ELECTIVE	Practice (5)
Bookkeeping with Business	Stenography (5)
Practice (5)	Typewriting (5)
Stenography (5)	Commercial Geography
Typewriting (5)	(½ year) (5)
	Economics (½ year) (5)

SESSIONS

The forenoon session opens at 8.30 o'clock and lasts until 11:45. The morning is divided into four periods of 45 minutes each for recitations.

The afternoon session begins at 1:10 o'clock and lasts until 3:25 o'clock. This time is divided into three periods.

STUDY

Pupils taking four studies of five recitations per week, or their equivalent, have two hours, generally the afternoon periods, for study. During this time they are expected to study two lessons. The remaining lessons are to be prepared at home. It is expected that two hours will be given to the preparation of the remaining studies. Pupils who take more than four studies have less time for study in school and consequently must employ more time in preparation of their work at home.

EXEMPTIONS

Any pupil receiving an average grade of ninety per cent or over, in any subject for the term is exempt from the term examination in this subject.

COURSES

The High School has three courses:—The College Preparatory, The General, and the Two Years Commercial Course.

The work of the College Preparatory Course is so arranged that the student may by proper selection of subjects fit himself for any college. As the entrance requirements of the various colleges differ materially, great care must be exercised in the selection of studies. Catalogues of the leading colleges are on file in the Principal's Office. These should be examined before making final choice of electives.

The work of the General Course is designed to give the student a general education or to fit him for a business career. This course should be taken by those who do not expect to go to college.

The College Preparatory and the General Course may be completed in four years. For this work a High School Diploma is granted.

The Two Year Commercial Course is intended for those who do not care to remain four years in the High School. It is planned in this course to give two years of stenography with one of bookkeeping, or two years of bookkeeping with one year of stenography. For this work a certificate is given but no High School Diploma is granted.

The management of the school will be pleased to confere with both parents and pupils concerning the choice of courses and electives.

The five courses offered at the high school were explained in the manual for 1917-1918, (below).

HIGH SCHOOL

The High School has five courses:

THE CLASSICAL,

THE TECHNICAL,

THE NORMAL,

THE COMMERCIAL,

THE GENERAL.

All girls who expect to go to a Women's College, all boys who expect to be lawyers, ministers or physicians or intend to take a classical course in college should take the Classical Course in the High School.

The Technical Course is intended for the students who expect to take up Engineering, Agriculture, Forestry, etc.

The Normal Course is intended for the students who expect to enter a normal school after graduation from the High School.

The Commercial Course is designed for students who expect to enter commercial life after graduation.

The General Course is intended for those who do not expect to go to college or who do not care to take up commercial work after graduation.

In addition to the five courses of the High School, enumerated above, a Two Years' Commercial Course is offered. This course is arranged for commercial students who cannot stay longer than two years in the High School. No High School diploma is granted for the completion of this course; however, a certificate is awarded, showing the amount of work completed.

GRADE NECESSARY FOR PROMOTION

The grade necessary for promotion is a general average of 75 per cent. with no branch with an average below 70 per cent.

Pupils who have been two years in one grade may be promoted at the discretion of the principal at the beginning of the third year, if the test warrants such promotion.

PROMOTIONS

All promotions will be made at the first and middle of each term. Pupils who are found to be in advance of their classes or behind their classes may be replaced at any time by the principals.

REQUIREMENTS FOR ENTRANCE TO THE HIGH SCHOOL

All pupils desiring to enter the High School shall be required to have completed the work prescribed for that grade and to be recommended by the teachers and principal as having completed the assigned work and to be fitted to do the work of the High School. Each pupil thus recommended will be given a promotion card setting forth the facts, which card will be necessary for admittance to the proper class in the High School. Certificates from other schools will be accepted when satisfactory to the Principal of the High School and the Superintendent under the direction of the Board. When such certificates are not satisfactory an examination may be given to afford the principal an opportunity to know where to place such pupils in the High School.

Athletics in 1911

In 1911 Wilkinsburg High School offered opportunities for athletes to participate in football, baseball, track and basketball.

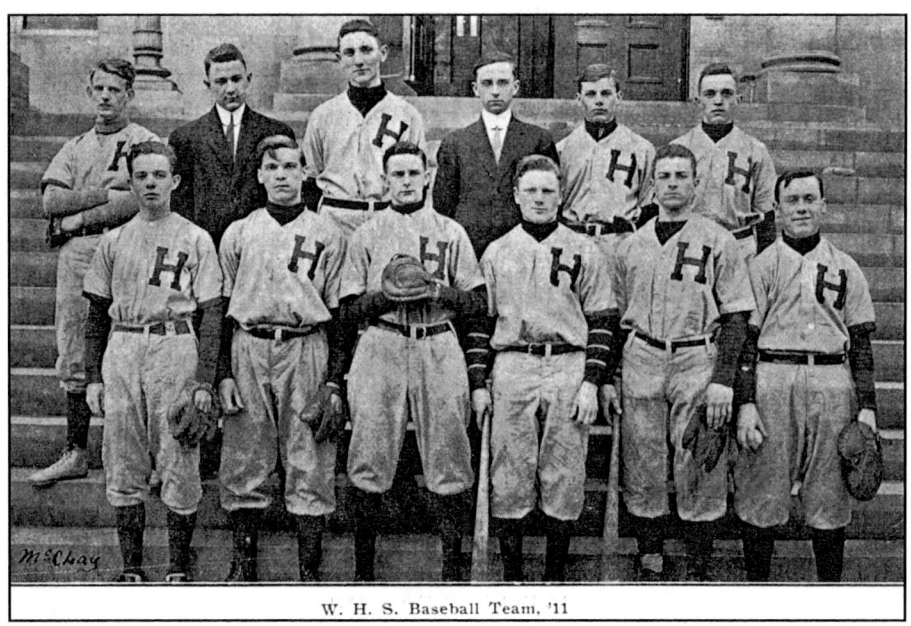

W. H. S. Baseball Team, '11

The WHS athletes used the Duquesne Country and Athletic Club Park which was located in the Hill-North-Pitt-Hay block.

The 1910-1911 Wilkinsburg track team was under the leadership of Mr. J. H. Edgerton.

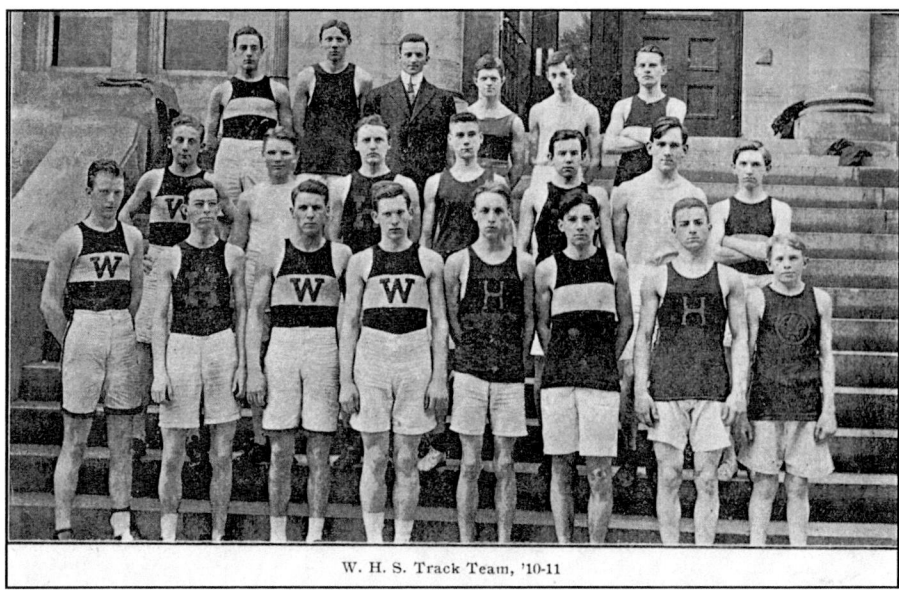

W. H. S. Track Team, '10-11

Wilkinsburg High School has always been a leader in clean athletic sports. Coach William Marshall directed the WHS football team in 1914, which brought us our first Western Pennsylvania Championship. Our team again won the WPIAL Championship in 1915 and in 1916.

The 1912-1913 basketball team showed extraordinary strength. The team won the Interscholastic Championship of Western Pennsylvania and the handsome silver loving cup offered by the Athletic Committee of the University of Pittsburgh.

The 1914 WHS track team displayed six trophies earned during an excellent season.

1912-1913 was the first year for organized basketball for WHS girls. Games were played with all the local schools and several college teams. This team broke even in its games with a record of five won and five lost.

In 1912 WHS introduced Physical Culture class for girls. This meant that all girls could participate in a gymnasium class. The girls were given two days out of the week in the gym, and the boys had the other three days.
This image shows the senior girls in 1912.

The 1919 Girls basketball team had a successful season with ten wins and only one loss. The girls won their games over Bellevue, Oakmont (twice), Sewickley, Alumni, Crafton, Schenley, Duquesne, Peabody and New Castle. Their loss was an away game at Peabody. These WHS girls gained the reputation of being very tough competitors.

The 1924 Girls basketball team had a successful season with thirteen wins and only one defeat. The team scored 218 total points over the competition. These WHS girls had a well-founded claim to the Championship of Western Pennsylvania.

Wilkinsburg High School possesses several trophies presented by the Syracuse Club of Pittsburgh, to the best Scholastic Football Team in Western Pennsylvania. Pictured is the WHS Football Squad of 1915, Interscholastic Champions of Western Pennsylvania.

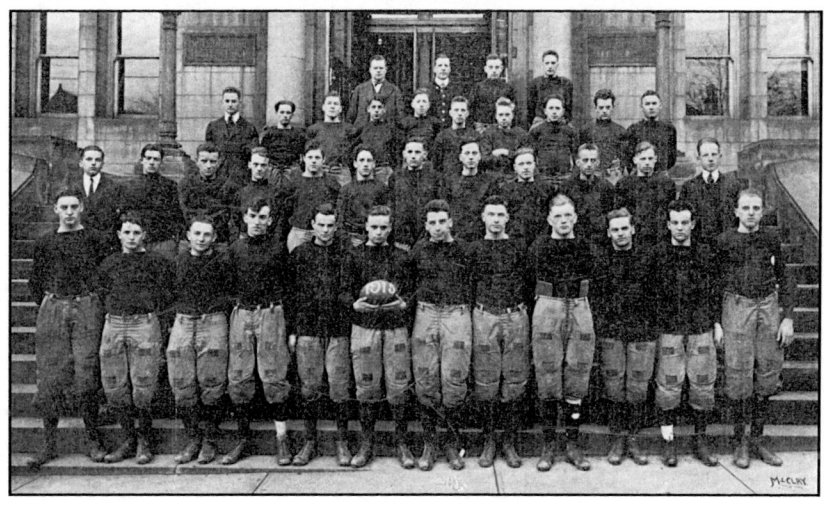

1915 Wilkinsburg High School baseball team, coached by R. G. Caldwell

1917-1918 WHS tennis team, under Coach Frank Ankeney succeeded in winning a championship. This was duplicated in 1919 with another winning season.

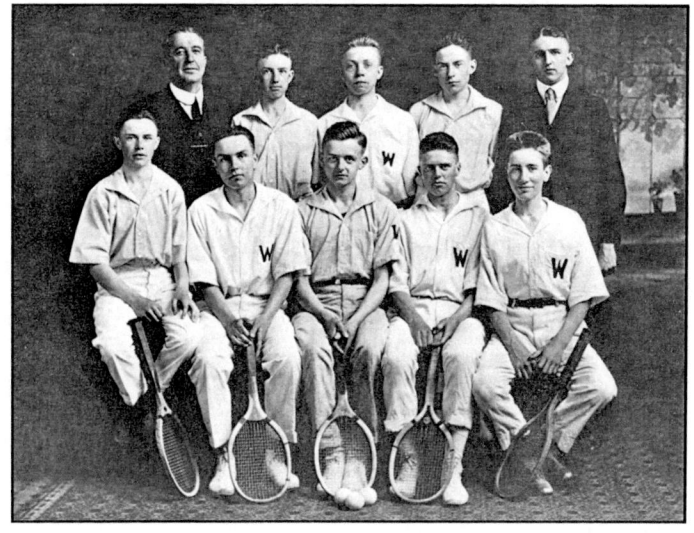

1918 boys track team had a very successful season. Four trophies were won and are proudly displayed. W.E. Eberts was the coach.

Scholastic Inc. founded by WHS student Maurice Richard Robinson

Maurice Richard Robinson

"Mose"

Class Treasurer (1); Class President (2)
(3) (4); Assistant Manager Football
(3); Athenian Literary Society (2)
(3) (4), Vice President (3), Critic
(4); Class Play (4); Inter-Society
Contest (3); Peabody Inter-scholastic
Contest (4); Editor-in-Chief "Review"
(4)

Maurice Richard Robinson, class of 1915, was one of WHS' most accomplished students. As a class officer every year, and as class president for three years, he shouldered many responsibilities, including being assistant manager of the football team. He was a member of the Athenian Literary Society, a critic for the class play, a member of the Inter-Society Contest, the Peabody Inter-Scholastic contest and editor-in-chief for the "Review."

Maurice Robinson attended, then graduated from Dartmouth in 1920. Robinson loved sports and journalism. In 1920 he created the *Western Pennsylvania Scholastic,* a publication he printed from the family home on 715 Wallace Avenue. This was the start of *Scholastic,* a company which eventually became the largest publisher of children's books in the world.

This is the very first edition of *'The Western Pennsylvania Scholastic,'* a weekly publication of school athletic events in the area. The first, October 22, 1920, was four pages long, but note that all others were eight pages long. Within two years the name was changed simply to *'The Scholastic'* to include a wider readership.

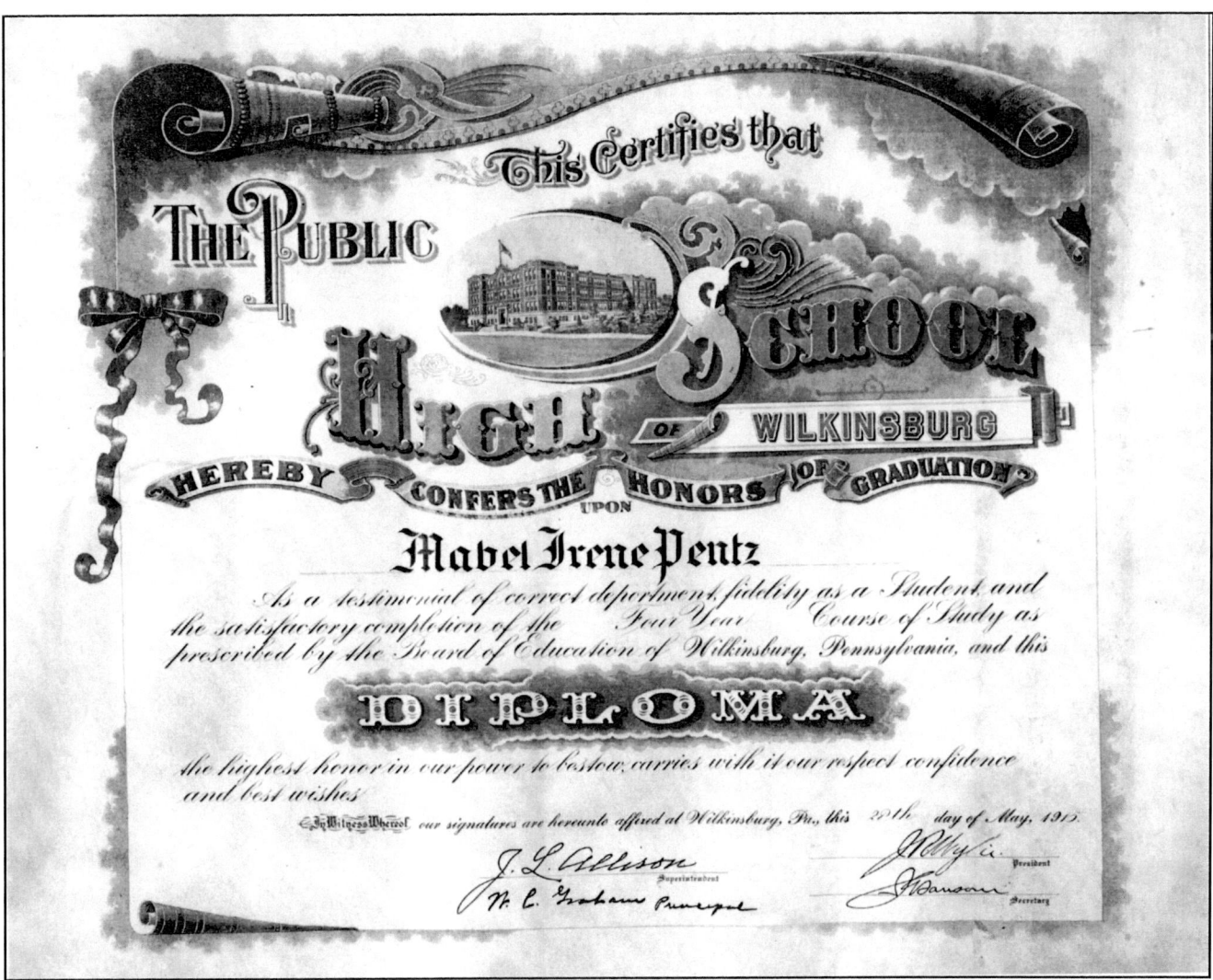

In 1915 the Wilkinsburg High School diploma was a huge document, measuring 22 inches wide and over 16 inches tall. In the center was an etched image of the high school. The printed diploma stated:

This Certifies that The Public High School of Wilkinsburg hereby confers the honors of graduation upon Mabel Irene Pentz as a testimonial of correct deportment, fidelity as a Student, and the satisfactory completion of the Four Year Course of Study as prescribed by the Board of Education of Wilkinsburg, Pennsylvania, and this Diploma the highest honor in our power to bestow, carries with it our respect, confidence and best wishes, In Witness Whereof our signatures are hereunto affixed at Wilkinsburg, Pa, this 29th day of May, 1915.

The diploma was signed by J.L.Allison, Superintendent (for whom Allison School was named), W.C.Graham, Principal, J.R. Wylie, President of the School Board and J. Sansom, Secretary of the School Board.

From 1911 until 1922 the WHS band received no financial aid from the School Board and provided their own instruments and music. They also did not receive credit for band, as orchestra members did. In 1922 the band finally received the backing of the School Board and their own uniforms. Thereafter, the band took part in every home football game, and was invited to play at the Washington game at Forbes Field. Twenty-four band men in uniform received an ovation from the thousands of spectators at Forbes Field. This image shows the 1922-23 band with Fred M. Bennett as Director.

Cheers from the *WHS Cheer Book*, 1915-1916

Hiffety, Heffety, Huss,
The point we'll not discuss,
But nevertheless, we'll just suggest
There's nothing the matter with us.

Hoo-rah, Hoo-rah, Hoo-rah Ray,
Wilkinsburg High School wins today.
GO ------High School
GO-------Wilkinsburg
Rah, Rah, Rah Team

Fight boys, we need a touchdown,
We are all here for you,
Root boys, for dear old High School,
Shout our colors - Red and Blue;
Backfield don't make a fumble,
Linemen do your best,
All your faithful friends will do the rooting,
If you'll do the rest.

Onward High School, Onward High School,
Plunge right thru that line,
Run the ball clear round
Touchdown sure this time.
Onward High School, on to victory,
Fight on for her fame:
Fight, fellows, fight and we will win this game!

"For You High," traditional school song for almost a century

Halsey Burdette Gilmour, who wrote the undying lyrics for the School Song of the Wilkinsburg High School, entered that building as a freshman in 1914. He wrote "For You, High" in 1915. Stricken with scarlet fever, he was absent from school for almost a year and recuperated at an area farm. In his high school years he was active in the Young People's Society of the United Brethren Church, and it was at that church that his mandolin orchestra practiced. He played in the WHS Band and Orchestra and in the Mandolin Orchestra. His instruments were the piano, mandolin, guitar and mandolin banjo.

Hal's song, "For You, High" took over in 1917 and it became the school song of WHS.

Hal was the son of Alfred Gilmour of 419 Campbell Street. Halsey returned to WHS for two years but he did not graduate, although he was only one credit shy of the mark.

World War One had started and he enlisted in the U.S. Army, choosing the 101st Cavalry combat Troop H. He was switched to the 107th Field Artillery, under Col. Charles McGovern and served in France with the American Expeditionary Forces. Hal was in a number of battles, was gassed by the enemy Germans thereby receiving four battle stars. The mustard gas poisoning caused him serious illnesses for many years after he returned to Wilkinsburg in May, 1919.

In May, 1922, he married Ruth Kintigh, a nurse in training at Columbia Hospital. Their ceremony was performed in the Second Presbyterian Church, now the Mulberry Presbyterian Church.

Hal and Ruth made their home in the 900-block of Rebecca Avenue with their four children. The writer of "For You, High!" died of pneumonia at the age of 30 in November, 1929 and is interred in Woodlawn Cemetery.

"For You, High!" is still played and sung at the football games and other athletic contests in which Wilkinsburg High School participates. Over the years WHS students have sometimes sung it with a plural phrase,"joys and glooms". It must be noted that Hal's original lyrics were "We'll share all joy and gloom."

For you, High, for you,
Our gallant red and blue,
We always will support you
In everything you do.
We'll share all joy and gloom,
Whatever comes to you;
And we'll always win our games
for you, High, for you, High.
We'll uphold your fame.

Graham Field - an addition to the athletic program at Wilkinsburg High School

Prof. William Graham, beloved as "Willie" to several generations of students, in 1915-1916 encouraged the School Board to purchase a large farm area on the Penn Avenue hill, the present Graham Field. This was done, a clearing of the land was started and the field was dedicated. This outstanding educator helped to organize the Western Pennsylvania Interscholastic Athletic League, and later served as its president.

For the 1916 football season the field was muddy with some semblance of being an athletic field. There was no grandstand, nor bleachers. Spectators stood to view the athletic contests, sometimes in mud up to their ankles. They cheered the Red and Blue teams and sang "For You, High!" The field became known as Graham Field by students and their elders and in 1917 the Board of Education officially gave it the name of Graham Field to honor the beloved school leader.

Pictured is the architects' plan in 1916 for the athletic field on Penn Avenue which resulted in the creation of Wilkinsburg High School's Graham Field.

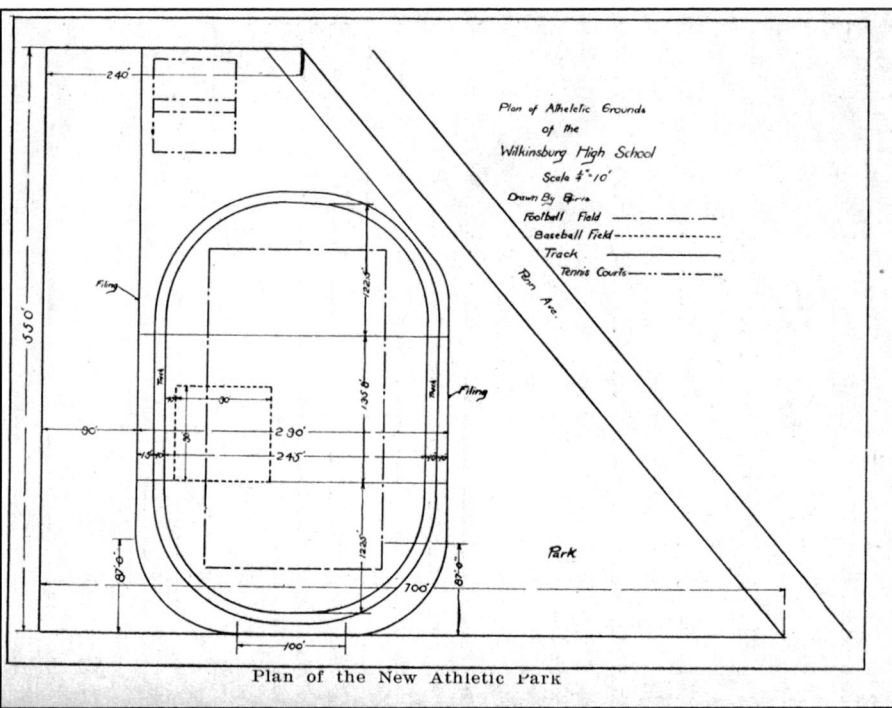

Plan of the New Athletic Park

The Grand Opening program for the Wilkinsburg Athletic Field started with a long street parade which began at the high school and marched up Penn Avenue hill to the new field. The program shows the Grand Opening at the corner of Penn Avenue and Weinman Street. Weinman Street was later renamed Princeton Boulevard. The day's events continued with performances by the Wilkinsburg High School Band, school cheers and songs with a finale of a football game between Homestead High School and Wilkinsburg High School.

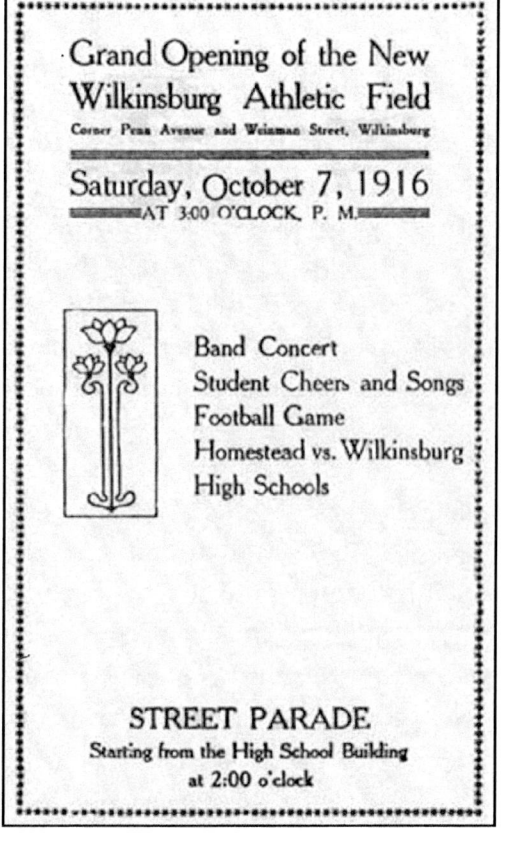

Grand Opening of the New Wilkinsburg Athletic Field

Corner Penn Avenue and Weinman Street, Wilkinsburg

Saturday, October 7, 1916

AT 3:00 O'CLOCK, P. M.

Band Concert
Student Cheers and Songs
Football Game
Homestead vs. Wilkinsburg High Schools

STREET PARADE

Starting from the High School Building at 2:00 o'clock

Grand Opening of the Wilkinsburg Athletic Field, Saturday, October 7, 1916

Place - the Johnston homestead on Penn Avenue, one square from the new Lincoln Monument

Size - Seven acres in the plot. Three and one-half acres graded for the field.

Features - Regulation Football Field; Baseball Diamond - One-fifth of a mile cinder running track - One hundred and twenty yard straightaway - Tennis courts.

Bleachers - Sixteen sections of college regulation bleachers, eight to twelve tiers high, sufficient seating space for several thousand people.

Fence Two thousand feet of chain link fence.

Cost - Original cost of property paid by the School Board $16,000. Debt assumed by the High School Athletic Association for grading and farming field, constructing running track, laying out tennis courts, building shelter houses, purchasing bleachers, erecting fence, etc. $8,500.

Entrances - The field has one gate at each of the four corners. The most convenient entrance for pedestrians is located at the lower corner on Penn Avenue. The entrance for automobiles is located at the corner of Penn Avenue and Weinman Street.

Maintenance - The Athletic Association, then the School Board paid the caretaker's salary. Additionally, the School Board erected his home, a very attractive six-room bungalow, pictured here.
The Track house is equipped with all modern conveniences which include showers, dressing rooms and combination lockers.
Graham Field is a benefit to the community as a place for recreation with its spacious field and tennis courts. It is such a well-equipped, beautiful field, and we are justly proud.

Graham Field track house in 1916

Graham Field tennis courts in 1916

Caretaker's bungalow in 1916

In 1916, the same year Graham Field was dedicated, the WHS football team won the WPIAL Championship and the Syracuse Trophy. This was the third time that Wilkinsburg had won the Western Pennsylvania Championship, having won in 1914 and 1915 as well.

The coach was William G. Marshall.

1922-1923 WHS tennis team had a successful season under manager Robert Swisshelm and Coach James V. Mates. Their home courts were located in Graham Field.

The new grandstand, built in 1928-29, could seat two thousand people and was roofed over for protection from rain and snow. In the space below the grandstand proper, (a space about two hundred feet long by forty wide) provisions were made for all activities connected with Graham Field. There were two separate locker rooms, shower rooms, storage area, and a large room for the Athletic Director, spacious enough for blackboard drills. When first constructed the roof spelled out *GRAHAM FIELD*, later changed to *WILKINSBURG*.

The 1921-22 boys' basketball team had a successful season, with a record of twenty wins and four losses, winning the Western Pennsylvania Interscholastic Athletic League championship.

The year 1922 was unique in that two W P I A L championships were won, one in football and one in basketball.

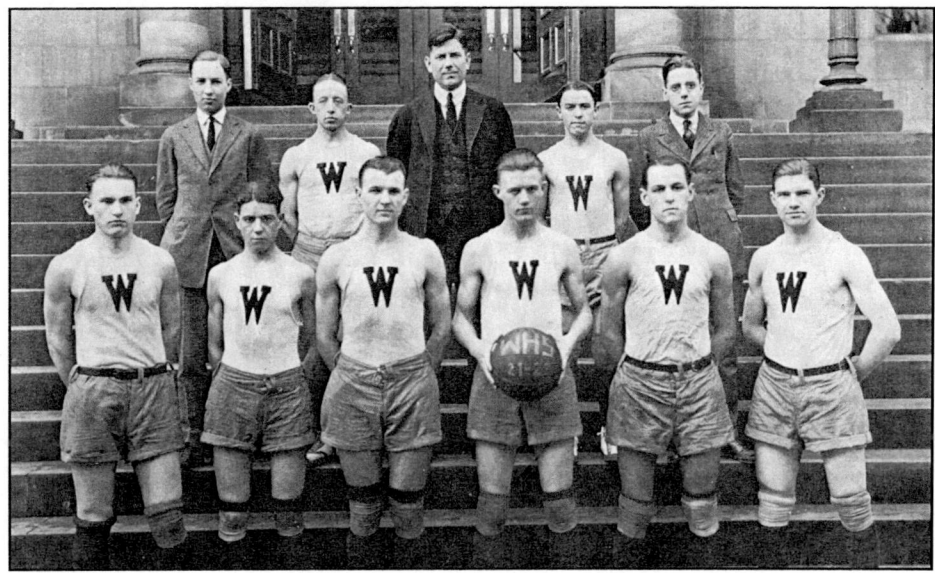

Wilkinsburg High School's 1923 track team posed in front of the track house at Graham Field. Their coach was Harry M. Springer.

Baseball, the national pastime, was a spring favorite at Wilkinsburg High. The high school baseball season started in April and lasted through May. The schedule included ten league and three exhibition games. The 1923-24 WHS baseball team exhibited keen competition and sparkling play under the direction of coach Leon E. Hoke.

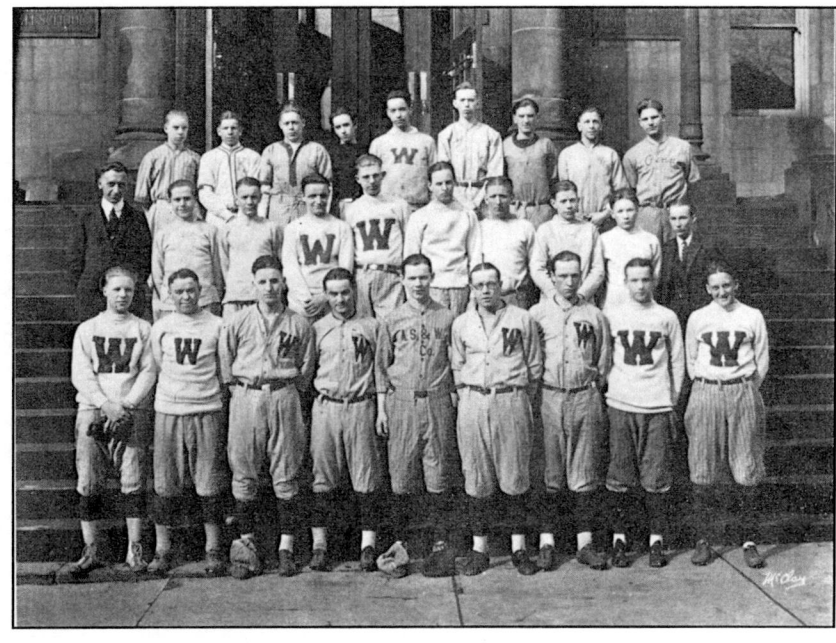

Through the playing of folk and classical music of many countries the orchestra gave WHS students an opportunity to learn the interests of other people and to appreciate fine instrumental music. It became an important part of chapel with its playing of the daily music. This image shows the WHS orchestra of 1918-19.

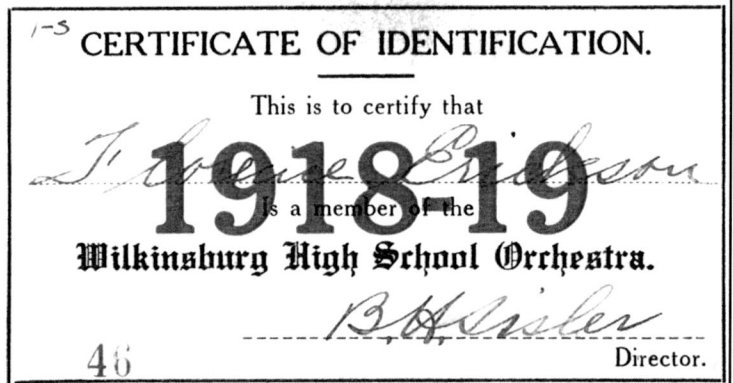

The WHS orchestra, entertained the student body, parents, and teachers in concerts throughout the year. The orchestra played for the daily chapel, operas, Christmas programs, the spring play and the commencement exercises. The orchestra had a fine reputation and was in demand for performances at community events and at local churches. The WHS Orchestra members were issued ID cards. This one belonged to Florence Erickson.

In 1922-23 the WHS orchestra had many talented student musicians. They performed with the drama department and during the Christmas season they gave two more fine performances - one at the vesper service and the other at chapel. In May the group played the traditional "Pomp and Circumstance" at Commencement.

The Activity Board was established in 1914 for the purpose of supervising school activities. The Board consisted of nine members, four members of the faculty and five students. Their main duty was to take charge of the money secured from school productions, plays, gym exhibit, musical concerts, and school dances. The Board managed the revenue, and planned the expenditures of this money to the best advantage of the organizations of WHS. This image shows the 1923-24 Activity Board.

The High School Review was published by the WHS students from 1905 to 1921, five times a year or more. The last or Commencement Issue of the Review each year served to honor the graduating seniors.

The *WIL-HI-SCAN* was the new yearbook for 1922, its only year. The name was changed to the *Annual* in 1923 and finally the *Tiger's Paw* in 1989.

The 1924-25 faculty posed for this photograph at the side of WHS. In the middle of the group stood Mr. William Graham, principal of the high school from 1903 to 1928.

The Wilkinsburg High School football team of 1921-22 was the most successful one since the championship team of 1916. Out of nine games played, seven were won, one tied and one lost.

By the 1922-23 season the football squad under Coach Harry Springer won all games played, and added the Syracuse trophy to our growing collection, by defeating Washington High School in a brilliant game played at Forbes Field.

Our gridiron warriors of 1922 gained the championship of the W.P.I.A.L. and the state championship as well. Pictured here are the "Champions of Pennsylvania" in an undefeated season.

1926 football team only gave up 25 points all season. During the 1926-27 year they played nine games. In three games they gave up 6 points per game, and in one game they gave up seven points.

The size of the goal post and cross-bar was not standardized at that time.

1928 was the introduction of the brilliant red jerseys with the large blue W and white numbers. These made the team quite conspicuous and they had eight glorious victories and one moment of defeat that year. They were the first team to use the new grandstand, showers and locker rooms at Graham Field. Elmer Carroll was the coach of the team.

1928-1929 A massive addition included a new gymnasium and auditorium for WHS

In 1929 an addition, commonly referred to as 'the annex' was opened. It virtually doubled the size of the facility. The design of the annex was unique in that a large gymnasium was placed on the third floor on top of a magnificent 1600 seat theater-style auditorium.

Auditorium entrance on North Avenue

North Avenue view of the entire addition

October 24, 1929 Rededication of the Senior High School

Dedication Since a nation, a state, a community cannot rise above the standards of its citizenship, since those standards are promoted only through education in its broadest and fullest sense, and since the foundation of such education is laid in its public schools, no greater challenge can come to a community than that of securing for the training of its young people every available educational facility.

Once again, Wilkinsburg has accepted this challenge by providing a high school, both in its handsome addition and in the rearrangement and redecoration of its old, second to none in attractiveness, adaptability and equipment.

To the development of a finer, nobler, more efficient manhood and womanhood for service to humanity at home and abroad, this splendid building is dedicated. May the blessing of man and God crown its efforts and its achievements.

Old Building - (built in 1911)
Basement: Cafeteria, boiler rooms, fans and girls' gymnasium.
First floor: Directors' room, office of superintendent, office of principal, office of secretary of School Board, seven class rooms, auditorium, two dressing rooms, two lavatories
Second floor: Teachers' rest room, library, nine class rooms, balcony of auditorium, two dressing rooms, two lavatories.
Third Floor: Two typewriting rooms, four domestic science rooms, chemistry laboratory, physics laboratory, biology laboratory, two laboratory offices, three class rooms, two lavatories, science lecture hall

New Building - (built in 1929)
Basement: Auto shop, electric shop, wood shop, large store room, vault, fan rooms and boys' lavatory.
First floor: Auditorium, two dressing rooms, office of assistant principal, four class rooms office of dean of girls, and nurses
Second Floor: Three class rooms, study hall, girls' lavatory, two dressing rooms and balcony of auditorium.
Third Floor: Three class rooms, boys' gymnasium, two shower rooms, two locker rooms, store room, study hall and boys' lavatory.
Fourth Floor: Study hall

Center Avenue side
of the new addition

1929
New
cafeteria
and new
boys
gymnasium.

The new 1929
auditorium, facing
toward the stage is
viewed from the
balcony.

This view facing
toward the audience
shows the beautiful
auditorium.

This image shows the 1924-25 band wearing their sailor-style uniforms. They played at all of the WHS home football games and occasional away games. In 1927, for the first time, the school band accompanied the football team to all of its games.

This photograph shows the original 14 steps and original doors of Wilkinsburg High School before the renovation of the Wallace Avenue entrance.

In November 1928 the band posed in front of the newly reconfigured entrance on Wallace Avenue. The glass globes had been removed for safe-keeping, half of the steps had been removed and the entrance doors were shored up with lumber. This construction project was part of the new gymnasium and auditorium addition built at the back of the school.

The band members now wore sport coats with WHS shields on their breast pockets. The band members and the school had a completely new look!

How many steps to enter WHS?   The number changed in 1928.

When Wilkinsburg High School was built in 1911, there were over fourteen steps to climb before entering the building on Wallace Avenue. There was a large decorative arched pediment over the doorway, and the columns were very tall. Pictured below is the mid-year class of 1929 (scheduled to graduate in January 1929), before the entrance and stairs were changed.

MID-YEAR 1929

In 1928, while the auditorium/gymnasium addition was being built, WHS remodeled the Wallace Avenue entrance. The decorative pediment was removed, three windows were added above the doorway, the columns were shortened, and the top six stairs were removed as the entrance was lowered. The lamp standards were reset at the lower level. Pictured below is the mid-year class of 1930 (scheduled to graduate in January 1930) after the entrance and stairs were changed.

Birth of the Tiger in 1929
Wilkinsburg High chose a symbol of its fighting spirit!

List ye, students, and you shall hear
Of the mascot that we all hold dear!
'Tis the High School Tiger, just born this fall
Yet for cunning and courage he surpasses them all.
As he strides on the field, all our friends have to cheer
But our enemies tremble and grow cold with fear.
And as the "Red and Blue Cyclone" sweeps down on the foe
That tiger is eager and ready to go;
And whether it's victory or disaster complete
Our tiger is never bowed down by defeat,
For he represents the spirit of Wilkinsburg High
Which is fight to the last and never say die!

In 1929 cheerleaders all were male in this Graham Field image, the first year for the WHS Tiger.

Chapter 4 - Athletics and Academics, 1930-1949

In the 1930s and 1940s Wilkinsburg High School continued to have a well-established reputation for athletic achievements and educational excellence. As Wilkinsburg's population grew, enrollment increased as did the variety of electives and sports.

1932 Wilkinsburg High School Varsity Football team, with Elmer E. Carroll as coach.
The season recorded seven wins, one loss and one tie.

Student Clarence Vogel posed as the WHS Tiger in 1932.

Wilkinsburg High School had only male cheerleaders until 1950. This image shows the 1932-1933 cheerleaders at Graham Field.

"Sound of the Drums" Wilkinsburg High School Marching Band thrills everyone!

1932-1933

The boys in the 1932 band marched up Penn Avenue hill to Graham Field every Saturday afternoon during football season. Before the game, the band played while enthusiastic voices sang school songs. Between halves the boys in their blue and red uniforms formed intricate figures as they played our favorites. Elwood N. Scott was the Director.

1932

A special feature was that of forming the initial letter of the visiting school. After this the band formed the letter "W" which never failed to give a thrill to everyone. While in this formation the band played "For You High" and "Onward High School"

1933

In the early 1930s the WHS football team had a 'mascot', a youngster from the elementary school who wore the uniform and attended the games with the band. The Tiger was considered to be a 'symbol' of the fighting spirit of the athletes. In later years the child mascot was discontinued and the Tiger became the only team mascot.

What's in a name?

In 1928-29 a grandstand was constructed in Graham Field. The roof of the grandstand had the name GRAHAM FIELD painted on it.

From 1930 to 1937, pictures show no name on the roof, as the letters had been painted over with white paint. In this 1934 image of the WHS Tigers (6) playing against Schenley (0), the grandstand shows no name.

The years of having no name on the roof (1930-1937) correspond to those years that the Wilkinsburg Airport was in operation. The Wilkinsburg Airport was located on Graham Boulevard in the Blackridge part of Wilkinsburg. The name removal might have been done to prevent early aviators from confusing the two fields, as they were less than a mile apart.

In this 1936 aerial view looking west, the long roadway is Penn Avenue down hill into the Wilkinsburg business area.

In the mid 1930s Tiger fans watched a football game at Graham Field. Note that the grandstand was still nameless.

The name WILKINSBURG was painted on the grandstand roof in late 1937 and remained through the 1980s. This image was taken in 1956.

Activity Board in 1932 was composed of five teachers appointed by the principal and five students elected by popular vote from the entire student body. One praiseworthy act of this Board was the erection of a new memorial to the soldiers who represented Wilkinsburg High School in World War I.

1931-1932 Activity Board

Each Friday in 1930 the Wilk-Hi-Crier dispatched the school news. By 1931 the school newspaper was renamed the Hi-Ways. The Hi-Ways newspaper was the result of the work of many WHS students: reporters, writers, typists, printers, proofreaders, editor, publicity manager, business manager, and sales people. The newspaper staff had high standards and won national awards for excellence.

1931-1932 school newspaper staff

1935 Hi-Ways sales desk

In 1937 the Hi Ways received commendation from the journalism department of State College for its editorials, interviews, and cartoons, and in 1936 was given International First Award by the Quill and Scroll and second place rating by the National Scholastic Press Association.

Wilkinsburg High School students joined challenging clubs.

1934-1935 Aviation Club members with their Liberty airplane engine

In 1934 Aviation Club members discussed aviation of the present and the future and the possibilities of aviation as a vocation. However, not all their time was taken up with discussion, for the boys acquired a 12 cylinder "V"-type Liberty airplane engine. They studied the mechanism of the engine with the purpose of putting it into good working condition.

Chess Club was organized in 1920 for those who wanted to learn to play the ancient game of chess, and to provide another form of interscholastic competition - one that depended on mental rather than physical ability. The club is a member of the Western Pennsylvania Interscholastic Chess League. This 1938-39 chess club had a very successful season and hoped to win first place in the league.

WHS boys sports teams competed against other high schools and the University of Pittsburgh.

In 1932 boys varsity swimming meets were held with Kiski, Munhall, Carrick, Peabody, Butler, Duquesne and Westinghouse High Schools. The boys also competed against Pitt Freshmen.

1931-1932

1931-1932

For the first time in eight years, an athletic team of WHS came through a season undefeated. This fine record was established by the boys' 1932 tennis team. Eight matches were held with the outstanding W.P.I.A.L. contenders. Seven of the games were won outright, the last one, with Pitt's Freshmen, resulted in a tie.

Track meets are a survival of the ancient Greek games when great honor was bestowed upon the winner of each contest. Skill and stamina is required and most of the work is an individual affair except for relay races. This team, the 1933 "W" men track team, won second place in the Independent Borough Meet and placed men in both the WPIAL and Pitt meets.

1932-1933

1932 Boys Varsity basketball had a successful season with fifteen wins and eight losses. They played the Western Pennsylvania School for the Deaf, and won with a score of 46-42.

Nine victories and only three defeats were tallied as a result of the 1933 baseball season. Turner Field was the scene of many well-played games because of the good coaching and the earnest efforts of all who participated.

1935-1936

For the 1936 varsity track team the highlight of the season was the performance of Burt Aikman and George Poindexter in the Penn State High School (PIAA) meet. (Aikman is in the first row, fourth from the left and Poindexter is in the second row, eighth from the left.) Both set new records for high school boys in their respective events, Burt winning the 880 yard dash in 2 minutes and George taking the 100 yard dash in 9.7 seconds. To set such records brought honors to Wilkinsburg High School.

Wilkinsburg High School Usher Squad

The Student Council elected the members of the Usher Squad. To be elected a boy needed to be outstanding in courtesy, neatness, and one whom the students were glad to follow as a leader. 1936 was the first year for the boys to have uniforms. The handsome red and blue jackets, the shining buttons and crisp white collars added much to the dignity of the position as the ushers stood erect at every entrance. The Usher Squad was neither a police force, nor a hall patrol, but rather a reminder of the proper courtesy to be observed in chapel. Every school day they were on duty in chapel.

The ushers contributed to the welfare and prestige of WHS as they were the official representatives of the students to welcome guests. Whenever the school staged a play, presented a musical program, had open house, or a gym exhibit, it was the ushers who by their courtesy and pleasant manner put our guests at ease.

By the 1940s the Usher Squad had grown to include fifteen young men. It wasn't until 1960 that WHS included girls as 'usherettes'.

The Drama Club department was always in the forefront developing a play or two yearly for the students and the people of the community. The above scene is from the 1942 hilarious comedy "One Wild Night" under the direction of Miss Sara Parson. Earlier year productions in the 1920s were the operas "Pirates of Penzance" and "H.M.S. Pinafore." In the 1930s it was "Growing Pains" with the trials of adolescence on the stage and a 1938 play "The Boomerang", a love-cure prescribed by a young doctor.

William C. Graham introduced chapel, a daily event for over 50 years.

To thousands of WHS graduates chapel has been a well-loved institution. In 1911 when the high school was built, the principal, Mr. William C. Graham, believing that education includes more than learning to conjugate a verb or prove a theorem, started the custom of daily chapel. Here students, meeting with the faculty for a short period of reverence, learned a sense of responsibility as they worked in the projection booth, at the organ, on the stage crew and on the usher squad. Others developed dramatic and musical skill as they performed for their classmates. To many seniors the most important time of all was that moment when they stepped to the podium to read the Bible and lead the Lords's Prayer, for they had taken one more step toward leadership in the adult world.

J. Donald Cook in 1932 opening chapel at the tap of the gavel.

By 1934 the student body had grown and everyone could not attend chapel at the same time. Student Council proposed a solution to the chapel problem. A Sophomore Chapel was put into effect and for the first time in the history of WHS, two gavels were struck and two preludes were played simultaneously, one ceremony being enacted in the new auditorium and the other in the old.

Students gathered at ten o'clock for daily chapel devotions. This chapel meeting was in 1940.

Wilkinsburg High was well-known for its excellent music department.

A Cappella choir - The purpose of this choir was to cultivate an appreciation of fine music and a sense of refinement in the school. Organized in 1931, the fifty members were elected each semester by vote of the students. Within the school, the choir lent much to the beauty and inspiration of the daily chapel service. In 1934 the A Cappella choir won national recognition when it was chosen to represent Pennsylvania in one of six coast-to-coast broadcasts sponsored by the National Music Educators.

Christmas Concert is one of the big events of the year in the music department. The A Cappella choir sang a group of Christmas hymns of the church. Old Christmas traditions were enacted and then well-known songs such as "Silent Night" and "O Holy Night" were sung. The concert always ended with the traditional singing of the Hallelujah Chorus. This concert was Christmas, 1941.

Orchestra is one of the oldest and most prominent musical organizations of WHS.

Since 1911 the orchestra has greatly aided the success of operas, plays, chapels, class nights, commencements, and other social functions by providing entertainment for attentive audiences and musical education to the student members. Orchestra members in 1943-44 played in the orchestra 'pit', an area sectioned off along the stage.The 1940s orchestras often played patriotic music honoring World War II servicemen and women.

This 1942-43 orchestra was directed by Mr. Elwood Scott as the students practiced for
the Spring Music Festival. There were twenty-five string players in this group.

1938-1939

Strike up the band!

At football games, at pep-meetings, parades, public gatherings, and political rallies it is heard. Always ready to respond to such a request, our band has become a high spot in both the school and community. The stirring marches and school songs, along with our cheers helped to inspire the football team to its full share of victories. The band added color and spirit to pep-meetings each Friday. Community celebrations were marked by parades in which the band marched, played, and always drew a crowd.

These photographs are all from the 1938-1939 school year.

Drum Major, George Kintzing

Band member, Herbert Hartson

Band members in 1938 made a "W" with their trombones at Graham Field.

Wilkinsburg High School cheers from the 1930s and 1940s

Victory Song

Come let's give a rousing cheer for high,
Cheer until our voices reach the sky.
A yell or two for Red and Blue,
Our songs we'll sing, let's make them ring,
As we march on to Victory.
  Rah, Rah, Rah
When the team is trying hard to win
Everybody's shouting "Don't give in",
Fight, fight, fight for High School,
Cheer the team to Victory.

Loyalty Song

Dear Wilkinsburg High we'll be true
To our colors, the red and the blue,
Our banner we'll wave
And a pathway we'll pave
To the school of the brave
 Dear Old High.
We pledge our allegiance to thee
Our Honor and Fidelity,
And in years from now when asked
From where do you come?
We'll proudly answer dear
        Wilkinsburg High.

W-I-L-K-I-N-S-B-U-R-G

A name which stands for honor and loyalty
The red and the blue before us
Ever victorious,
We'll shout the chorus

When duty calls to the East and the West
We'll sing the praises of the school we love best
And may each son and daughter stand the test
And honor bring to W.H.S.

W-I-L-K-I-N-S-B-U-R-G
That spells victory!
W-I-L-K-I-N-S-B-U-R-G
That spells loyalty!
W-I-L-K-I-N-S-B-U-R-G
Ever Strong and True,
With your name and your fame
You will always remain
Our guiding light, dear Red and Blue.

1936-1937 cheerleaders

1934-1935 cheerleaders

For the boy who wanted to learn a trade or to enter an industry upon graduation, WHS offered a Mechanic Course of study. This course is the only one that had no electives. Over a three year period it included Industrial History, Shop Mathematics, Mechanical Drawing, Industrial Physics, and Chemistry, along with the three shops: Electric, Auto, and Wood, pictured here in 1939. The Electric Shop provided a firm foundation in the construction and application of electrical devices. In the Auto Shop a boy learned how automobiles were constructed and repaired. The Wood Shop included furniture design and construction.

1930-1931

1933-1934

1934-1935

1936-1937

1940-1941

Auto Shop was extremely popular with the mechanically minded boys. The shop was located in the basement of Wilkinsburg High School and was fully equipped with mechanics tools. Auto Mechanics was offered to WHS boys from the 1920s into the 1990s.

1924

Annual Field Day featured school physical education to the Wilkinsburg community.

Field Day was an annual outdoor demonstration of the physical education activities of all the Wilkinsburg schools from elementary through high school. It was held early in May to give the community of Wilkinsburg a general view of the work carried on throughout the school system. This image shows Field Day of 1937 at Graham Field with Frank C. Biddle directing the group singing.

The 1937 Field Day program included mass drills and group marching of students.

Annual Field Day also included a demonstration of the high school girls field hockey skills.

Girls intramural sports offered opportunity, variety and fun.

In the 1930s and 1940s the intramural athletic program at WHS offered many chances for extracurricular activities to all students not participating in varsity sports. In addition to the hours spent in gym classes, students could take part in additional basketball, volleyball, mushball, swimming, tennis, and fencing. In the 1930s WHS girls also had such activities as field hockey, modern dancing, hiking, and horseback riding, while the boys had intramural sports such as football, baseball, handball, and bowling. In 1939 soccer and ping-pong were added as other intramural sports.

These images were all taken in the late 1930s.

Boy's and girl's fencing teams won trophies to add to WHS' growing collection.

In 1939 the WHS fencing team brought honors to our school by winning the silver fencing cup at the Pittsburgh Fencing Club Tournament, held at the Pitt Stadium. At that time, the Pittsburgh Fencing Club was composed of eight teams, including the University of Pittsburgh. WHS had fencing teams from the mid-1930s to mid-1940s.

1937-1938

1938-1939

G

1938-1939

Gym Club at WHS featured athletic champions.

These images show the 1941-1942 WHS men's gymnastic team, the year they won the WPIAL gymnastic championship.

Gym Club members of 1942 brought exceptional honor to themselves and to Wilkinsburg High by capturing the WPIAL gymnastic championship.

In earning the title, the Red and Blue squad annexed championships in three events: parallel bars, rope climb and horizontal bar.

WHS had outstanding gymnastic teams during the 30s and 40s.

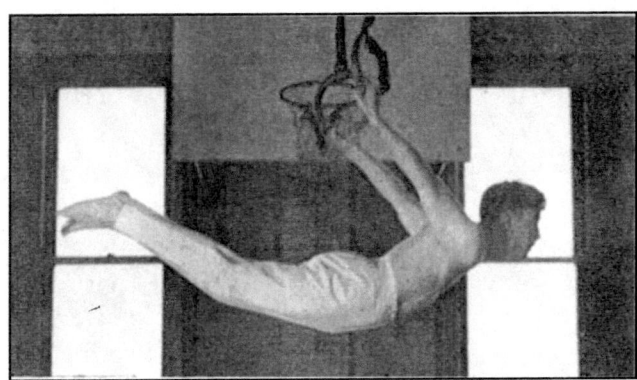 

These images show members of the 1938-1939 gymnastic team demonstrating skill on the rings and horizontal bar.

Cross Country 1945 team did well. Bill Kroske (second from the right bottom row) placed fifth in the W.P.I.A.L. Championship which qualified him to compete in the state championship meet. At Penn State he ran sixth in a field of fifty-seven contestants.

1944-1945 WHS Cross Country team

1945 season is the first one in eight years that WHS sponsored a baseball team. The team, coached by Harold B. Grimm, played their home games at Hunter Field and were encouraged by WHS enthusiastic baseball fans.

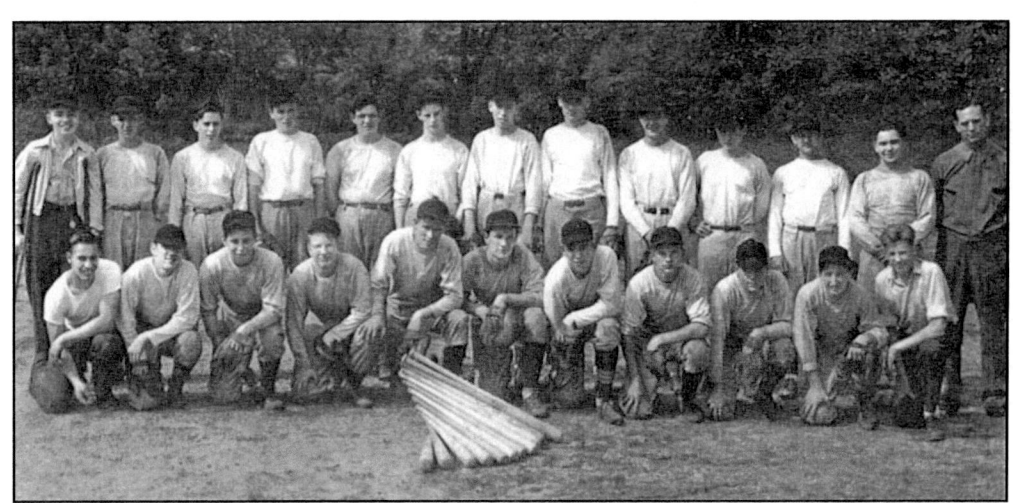

1944-1945 WHS baseball team
Coach Harold B. Grimm is on far right wearing a dark jacket

Wilkinsburg began a new era of athletics in 1946 with the installation of an excellent lighting system at Graham Field.

With Mr. Bill Lohr as head football mentor, the Tigers in their first game under the lights defeated Pitcairn. The Red and Blue walked off with a smashing 13 to 0 victory. Thus the Tigers chalked up the first one in the 'win' column of the 1946 season.

Tigers football team for the 1946-1947 school year.

There was always excitement at Graham Field!

1943 "W" in the field

1946 WHS Tiger at Graham Field

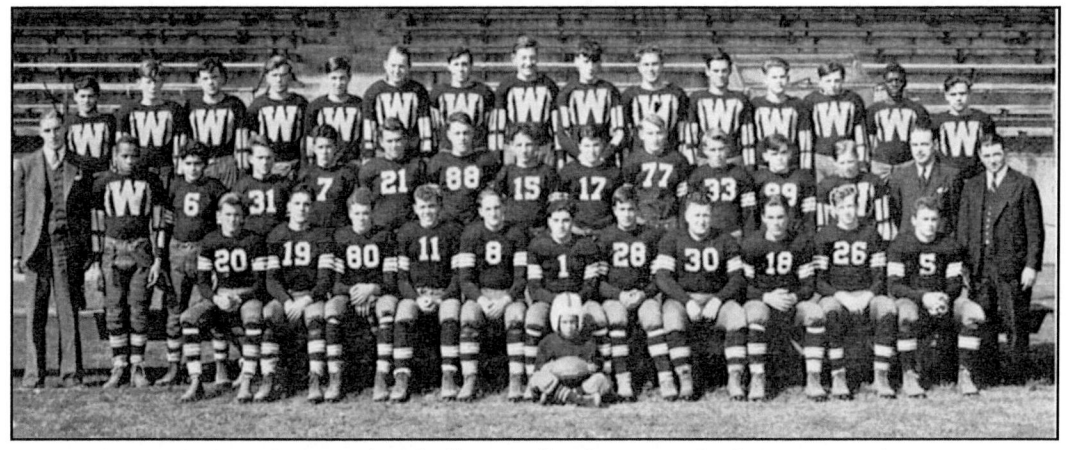

1938-1939 WHS Tiger football team had a record of 7 wins and 2 ties.

1948-1949 Color Guard

WHS scoreboard shows a 1948 victory.
Final score was: WHS 32, Latrobe 6

1948 "W" in the field, under the new lights

One of the best examples of teamwork ever to represent WHS was the gridiron juggernaut of 1942.

This unbeatable machine under the direction of Coach Karl Bohren and his two assistants Graydon Campbell and Herbert Creigh crushed nine foes as the 1942 outfit became Wilkinsburg's initial undefeated and untied eleven since 1926.

In 1946-1947 the WHS Varsity Club was in its third year of existence. Recognition was given to each wearer of the 'W' by his admittance into the Varsity Club. Membership in the Club indicated that each one had played in a minimum number of quarters in basketball or football, or innings in baseball, or had scored points personally in track, tennis, or golf.

The club sponsored the Varsity dance and the annual basketball game between football and basketball teams.

'W' presented to the lettermen was their reward for effort and achievement in athletics. It was a red chenille and felt varsity letter 'W' outlined in blue. When the lettered athlete became a senior, a navy blue wool sweater was an added honor.

Graduation at Graham Field in the '30s and '40s

In the early 1930s Wilkinsburg High School moved its commencement exercises from the school auditorium to an outside venue, Graham Field. This enabled more family members to attend since the seating capacity in the grandstand was twice that of the auditorium.

When the commencement program was finished, students recessed alphabetically to greet family members. Each graduate held proof of their achievement: the rolled up diploma secured with a red ribbon.

Flag bearers led the graduates in the commencement exercises at Graham Field.

Commencement included the Pledge of Allegiance, a selection of music from the WHS orchestra or band, an inspirational speech, awarding of honors, presentation of graduates, and awarding of diplomas. It concluded with a Benediction and a Recessional.

This Commencement Program was from the WHS class of 1941.

Commencement Program

Processional—"Knights of Chivalry" _____ Panella
High School Band

Invocation _____ Reverend George A. Parkins
Pastor of Ross Avenue Methodist Church

"Awakening" _____ Frances Austin
Senior Girls' Sextette
Jeanne Counsel, Jeanne Dorfman, Jeanne Follette, Jeanne Lorenz
Marjorie Little, Dorothy Swan
Piano, Marjorie Ricker; Flute, Ralph Phillips; Drum, Robert Precious

Theme:—The Land of the Free

Democracy—Our Heritage _____ Dorothy Geiger

Democracy—Our Obligation _____ Lois Allshouse

Pledge of Allegiance _____ Class of 1941

"Joy" _____ Cadman

"I Love Life" _____ Manna Zucca
Senior Chorus

Awarding of Honors _____ Mr. W. C. Graham
Superintendent of Wilkinsburg Schools

Alumni Award _____ Mr. J. Duff Mason
President of Wilkinsburg High School Alumni

Presentation of Class Members _____ Clifford Weisel
President of Class of 1941
Assisted by Jared Haines and Albert Kimball

Awarding of Diplomas _____ Mr. Harold S. Carmack
President of Wilkinsburg School Board
Assisted by Synthia Daw, Jean Dorfman, Mary Ann Church,
Jean Morse, Pearl Mason, and Patricia Werner

Class Song _____ { Words by Ruth Jane Colmery
                           { Music by Jean Lorenz

Benediction _____ Reverend George A. Parkins

Recessional—"Knights of Chivalry" _____ Panella
High School Band

The audience is requested to remain seated during the processional and recessional.
Graduates will be pleased to receive their friends following the recessional,
at the Penn Avenue side of Graham Field.

Majorettes

The 1946 football season meant the opening of a new era in school life as the first majorettes of WHS ushered the band down Graham Field. Wilkinsburg was grateful to these five young women, not only for the wonderful job they did in those brilliant red and white uniforms but also for successfully crushing the years of prejudice against majorettes. The students of Wilkinsburg will look back with gratitude for their pioneering school spirit.

1946-1947

The 1949 majorettes were a group of high-stepping, versatile young women who were very proud of the honor WHS had conferred upon them. They devoted long hours to practicing intricate drills and baton-twirling. The majorettes were attired in snappy red-and-white skirts with jackets and wore hats with large breeze-catching plumes.

1948-1949

In 1949 the WHS majorettes thrilled the students at the Friday Pep rallies.These majorettes also entertained at numerous functions held by local civic, school, and patriotic groups. During the school year they twirled for the Lions Club, American Legion, Kiwanis Club, Johnston, Semple and McNair Schools, the Lions Midget game and the Halloween parade.

1948-1949

This 1948-49 Tigers football team worked hard under coaches "Wild Bill" Lohr (last row, far left) and Jason Snyder (last row, second from left) These coaches showed a keen interest in the boys as well as in the sport. Through training them to win the game, they set high ideals of fair play, unselfishness and determination. This team ended the season with nine wins and only one loss.

The WHS Tiger was an energetic and enthusiastic leader of
cheers on the sidelines or at pep meetings in the late 1940s.

In 1948, under the excellent coaching of Mr. John Browning, the WHS track squad won the most coveted of all the district track honors, the WPIAL Championship. Bud Alcott tied the WPIAL high hurdles and set a new mark for the 200-yard low hurdles at 22.4 seconds.

Tom Stephens (first row, fourth from left) set another new record in the 180-yard low hurdles of 20.9 seconds. The mile relay team of Bell, Anderson, Morgan and Jaffurs placed second in the WPIAL meet.

1948-1949 WHS track team, WPIAL Champions

In the state meet George (Bud) Alcott won the 120-yard high hurdles in 14.9 seconds; he also won the 200-yard low hurdles in 22.2 seconds and placed second in the broad jump. Bud Alcott was named second on Look Magazine's All-Star Track Team for 1948 in running the 200-yard low hurdles.

George (Bud) Alcott had brilliant performances in 1948-1949.

The 1947-48 team continued in championship form by copping the Section VIII title. Meeting in the quarter-finals with Freedom, the Burg boys returned victoriously with a score of 65 to 43. Their 22 game winning string was cut by Ford City in the semi-final jinks. The students of WHS are truly proud of their outstanding athletes.

Wilkinsburg High School: Century of Learning, 1911-2011

Chapter 5 - WHS moves up in status, 1950-1969

Wilkinsburg getting into big time in 1952 to
become a second-class district, the third in Allegheny County.

Wilkinsburg got the word that it had grown up into a second-class school district, the third in Allegheny County. Before this time, only Pittsburgh and McKeesport had reached such status, limited to places of over 30,000 population. The 1950 census showed Wilkinsburg over 32,000, but state action to change its status was delayed until after official census rechecking.

The change to a second-class district became effective July, 1952. Second-class status required naming two additional school directors, and involved many features not required of third-class districts. Soon after the tentative census report of 1950, School Superintendent William M. Potter notified the Wilkinsburg School Board of the coming change. The Board, composed of nine members, represented the third largest community in Allegheny County, and twenty-fourth largest in the Commonwealth of Pennsylvania. Wilkinsburg rated among the best school districts for the educational program in effect and for the excellent facilities that were provided.

On the recommendation of Dr. Potter, the board launched a five year modernization plan of more than a million dollars, and built up its services to the required standard for a second-class district. Dr. Potter won the hearts of the students and realized the hopes of years in renovating the school plant: new lights in all six buildings, painting of all buildings inside and out, a new home economics department in the high school and a modern stage and redecorated auditorium. Getting in shape as one of about 25 second-class districts in the state, Wilkinsburg began its five-year plan with a cleanup.

William M. Potter

This 1950 image shows the high school during the steam cleaning of the brick. As steam cleared the years of grime from the dingy senior high school building, it emerged as a handsome structure of Flemish brick. Two others of the district's seven school buildings were cleaned, and work scheduled on the four others. The plan included a rotation arrangement to keep the buildings clean in the future.

Also launched was a modernization program which brought many changes. One of the first was a new $80,000 home economics department in the senior high school, a dream of color and modernity. The junior high school also got a new home economics department, and then the modernization of shops and art rooms. New lighting and wiring was also installed, of the latest type.

Health rooms were installed in each building, two of them complete hospital rooms with full equipment. Changes were made from the old type of fixed furniture to moveable pieces, to make for modern, social, classroom methods. Linoleum floors were put in to provide health guards and easy cleaning. Special teaching aids were added to supplement books, including new-type duplicating machinery, visual aid equipment, new library facilities, library improvements and other needs. The original 1911 auditorium had been transformed into the school library. In 1950 the library was renovated to provide better lighting, seating and access to books and educational materials.

Library renovation before the new lights were installed.

Ed Frech and Librarian Mrs. Margaret Neri in 1964. The improved lighting was installed in 1950.

At full strength for second-class status, the Wilkinsburg system included a 21 member administrative staff and 177 full-time professional employees. On the staff were seven principals, psychologists, school-home visitor, vocal and instrumental music directors, art director, business manager, two deans of girls, two guidance counselors, and others.

The 1952 year's budget was more than $1,350,000, of which $900,000 was for salaries. Wilkinsburg charged 18 mills school tax on about $43,000,000. with a $10. head tax for modernization funds.

Some 325 tuition students attended from corners of Pittsburgh, Wilkins (Churchill Borough and Forest Hills Borough) and Penn Townships, with their school districts paying about $80,000 annually.

The citizens of Wilkinsburg have selected some of their best men and women for the school board, including businessmen, corporation executives, and one minister. Perhaps none was happier at the new status than J. Donald Ferguson, a member of the board for 32 years, who watched the district grow from small beginnings to one of the most complete and modern in the state. (Ferguson playground and tennis courts were named in memory of Don Ferguson. They are located on the site of the former McNair School, corner of South and Center Avenues.)

Dr. William M. Potter, (left) Wilkinsburg School superintendent, headed all educational activities. Under his jurisdiction were five grade schools, the junior high school, and the high school.

As principal of WHS, Mr. Edward Ege (right) presided over chapel, was chairman of the Activity Board, and often acted as counselor to students. He was a 1915 graduate of WHS.

School administrators frequently held breakfast meetings in the Home Economic department.

Miss Gwynne Mothersbaugh was well known for her active part in school life. As the dean of girls for over two decades she helped WHS girls solve problems. Miss Mothersbaugh also planned schedules, sponsored the Senior Counselors, and assisted in social activities. Miss Mothersbaugh was an alumna of WHS, graduated in 1922.

Mr. Ernest Bishop wore many hats at WHS. He was the Industrial Arts teacher, then the guidance counselor. Mr. Bishop was a part of WHS life for over 45 years.

The **WHS Student Handbook** was distributed at the beginning of each school year. It included diagrams of each floor so new students could easily locate their classrooms.

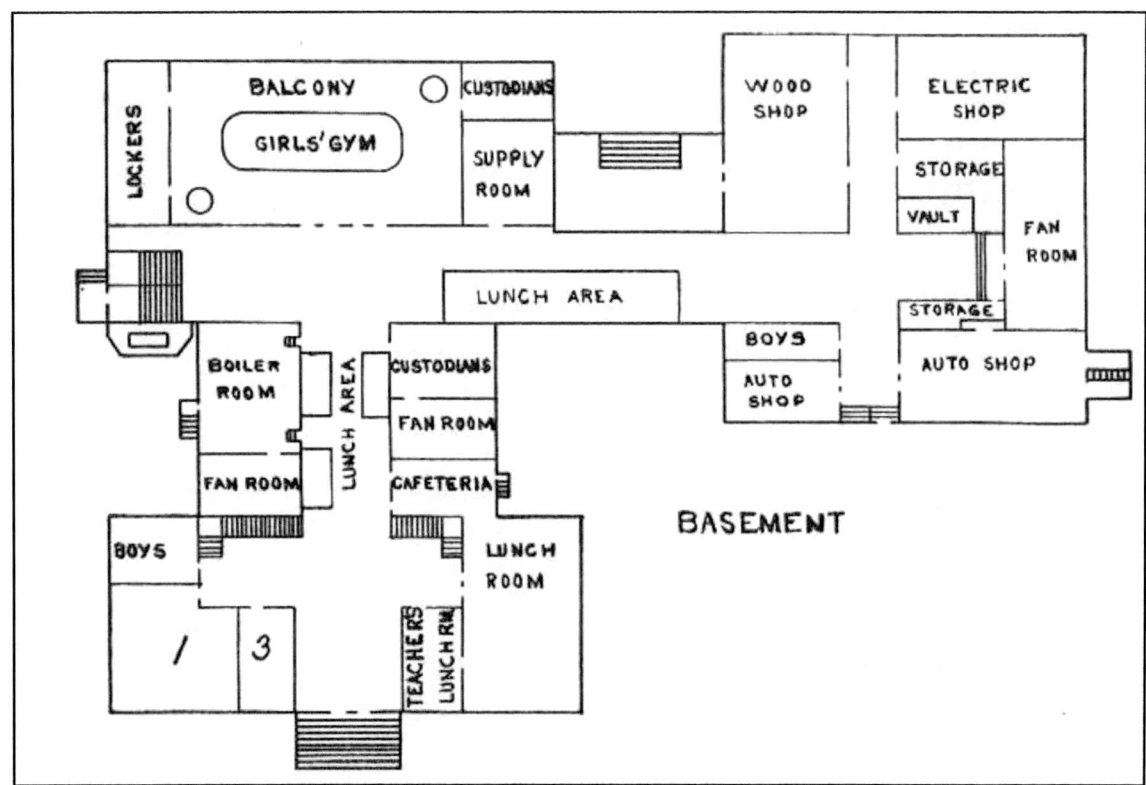

These floor plans were taken from the 1952 WHS Student Handbook.

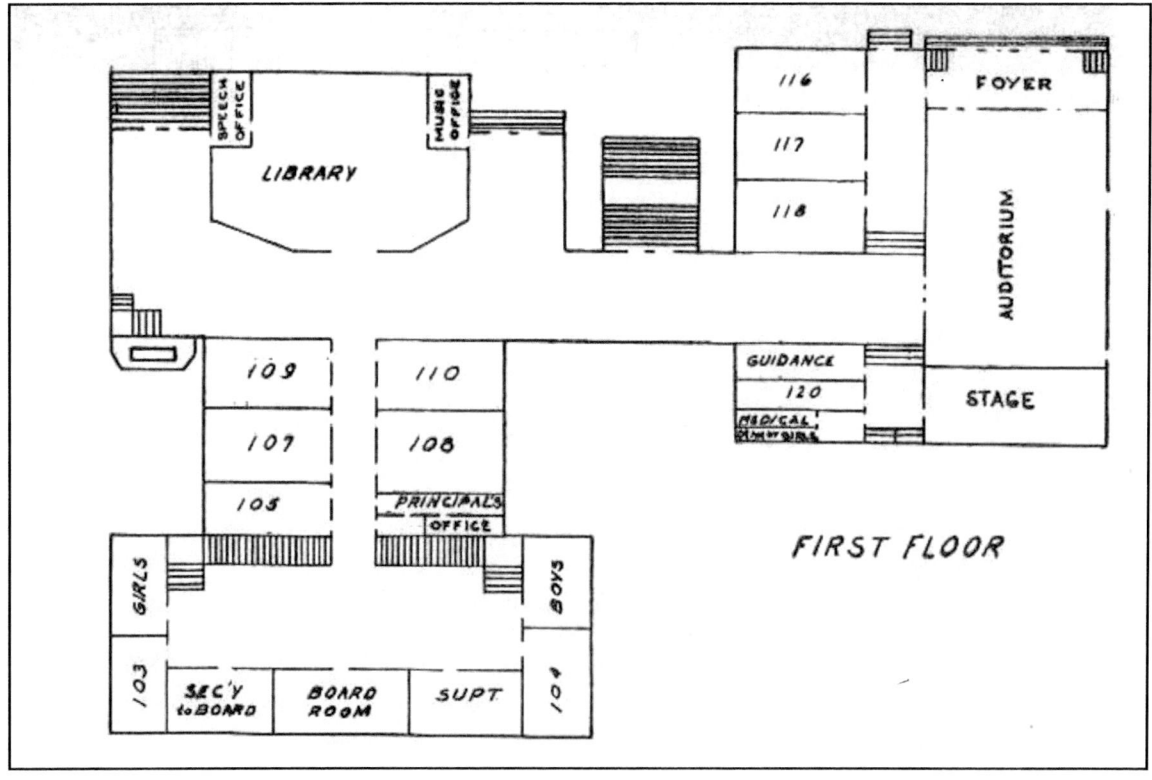

Wilkinsburg High School: Century of Learning, 1911-2011

Second and third floor plans are from the 1952 Wilkinsburg High School student handbook.

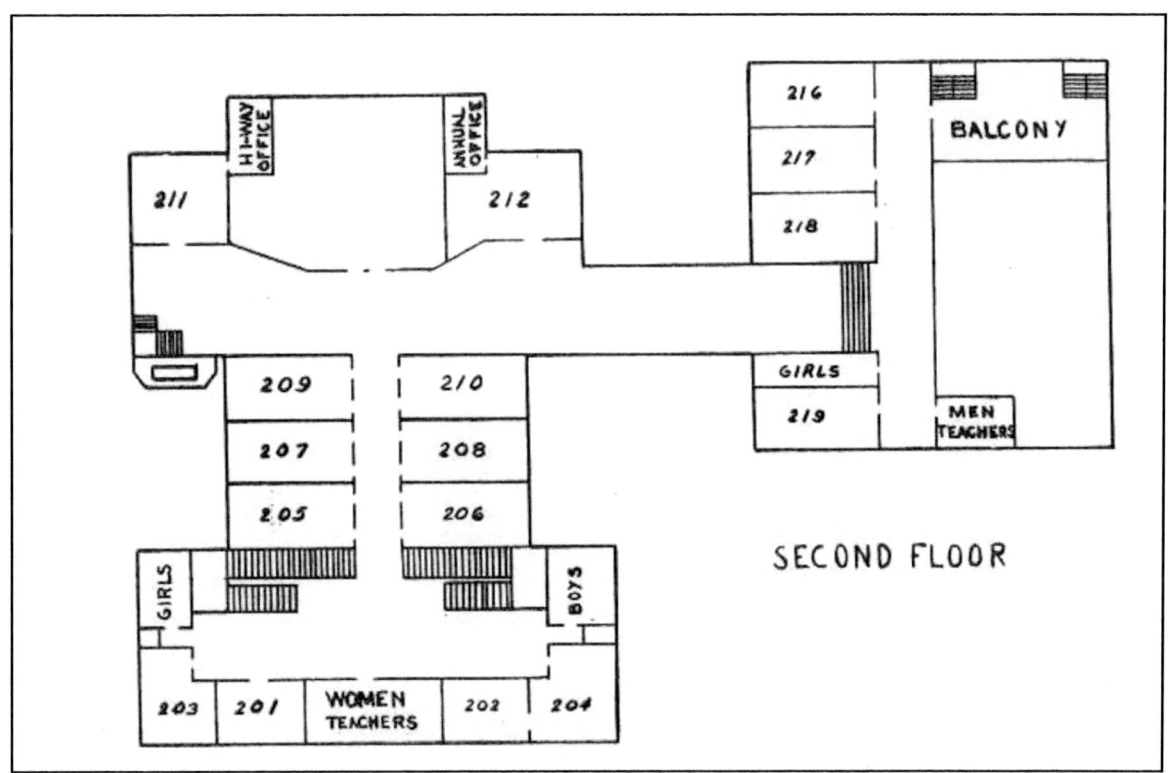

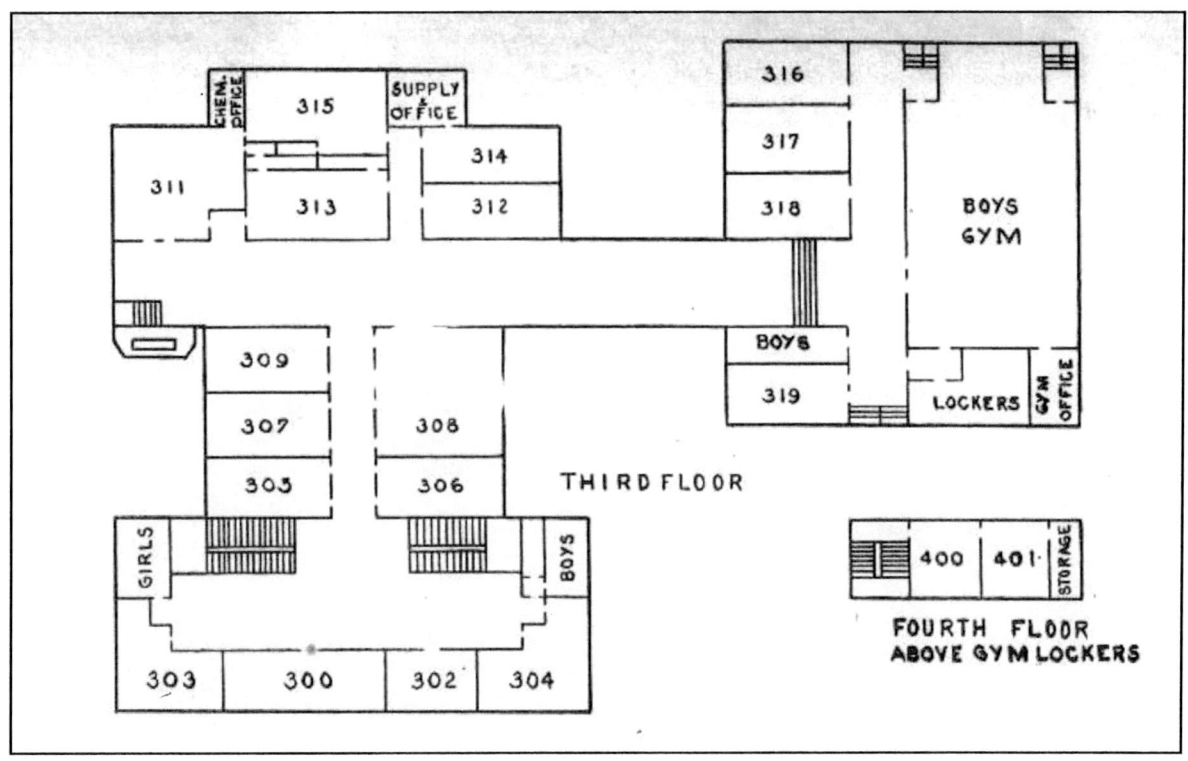

Students arrived at Wilkinsburg High from different areas and in varied ways.

1943 Forest Hills students pedaled home on their bikes. Other students traveled on the 87 Ardmore streetcar line.

1949 students are leaving WHS to walk home.

For over 50 years students came from Pittsburgh, Forest Hills and Penn Hills. These students had their school districts pay tuition to Wilkinsburg so that they could access the excellent educational opportunities that WHS had to offer. This image is from the 1952-1953 school year.

This 1962 image shows the Churchill school buses in front of WHS picking up the students from that area. Wilkinsburg, at only 2.2 square miles was geographically small enough that buses were not used for resident students. For Wilkinsburg residents it was considered to be a walking district.

Wilkinsburg High School: Century of Learning, 1911-2011

Receiving their class rings in 1955, WHS juniors admired the beautifully crafted symbol of their school.

A repeated theme over the past century is that Wilkinsburg High School students strived to bring honor to their school through academic achievement, athletic ability, musical talent in choir, band or orchestra and participation in community events. As representatives of WHS, students knew that outsiders may judge the school by the actions of the students. A Creed was developed and included in the WHS handbook so that each student knew what was expected of him or her. Wilkinsburg was praised often for the outstanding students and high quality of student life.

W. H. S. CREED

As a student of the Wilkinsburg High School I will endeavor:

1. To manifest a school spirit which will bring honor and respect to Wilkinsburg High School.
2. To be courteous, kind and thoughtful in and out of school, thus reflecting honor upon my school, my home and myself.
3. To keep my school and school property in such condition that it will be a pleasure to have others see them.
4. To conduct myself in the Hall, Class and Study Rooms in a manner becoming a lady or gentleman.
5. To act in such a way in Chapel that my reverence may add to the devotion and that my attitude will help to make the program successful. If you will make this creed, your creed, we are sure that your life will be happy and profitable and that you will bring honor to our Red and Blue.

Creed copied from the 1952 WHS student handbook.

1958 view of WHS from the Penn-Lincoln Hotel

Home Economics department was renovated in 1950.
WHS girls learned to sew, cook, weave, and manage a household.

Home Economics students made dumplings in 1951.

Home Economics Department, 1952

1956 baking cookies

1951 sewing class

1957 weaving bamboo mats

1963 baking class

1967 checking the recipe

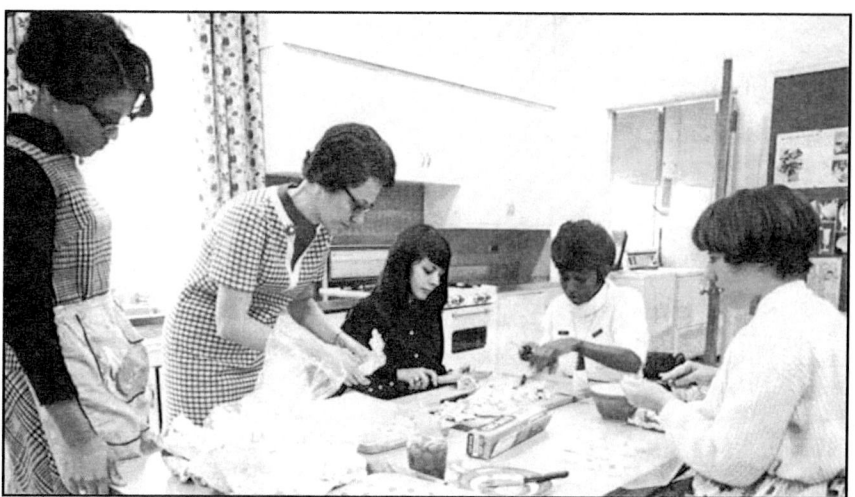

1969 baking class

Boys developed woodworking skills in the WHS woodshop class.

Creating a project for the elective woodshop class has been going on for over 75 years at Wilkinsburg High School. The students made both useful and decorative items. Here are some examples from the 1950s and 1960s.

In 1955 a woodshop student stabilized the legs of his custom-made table.

In 1956 student Don Pawlak began his woodshop project.

In 1957 Clark Lingren and Larry Shugerts built a boat in WHS woodshop.

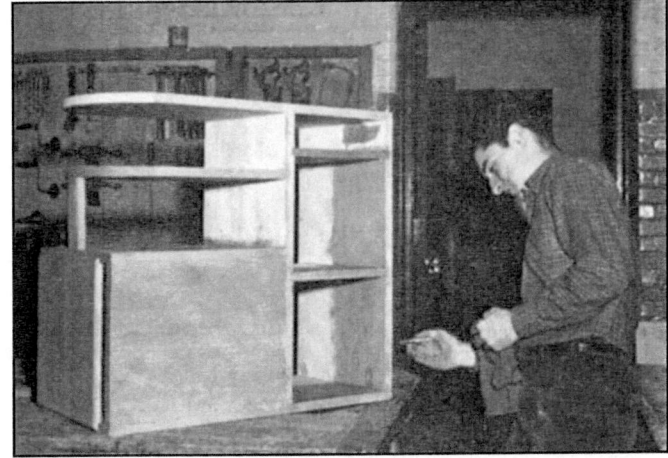

Putting the finishing touches on an end table he designed in woodshop is John Dougherty in 1958.

Pat Ryan and Ed Patalski built a shelf in 1963

This 1950-1951 Tiger band included girls, a new addition in 1950. The girls performed admirably and added greatly to the size of the band. The first annual band concert, a mixture of classical and popular music was very successful. Representing the WHS band at the Western District Band Concert at Millvale were Justin Johnson, Marlene Kammrath, and Harry Hellings.

A new Tiger Band marched onto Graham Field at the first WHS football game in fall, 1952. This band had twelve majorettes, six more than before. Resplendent in their new uniforms, the band performed difficult precision drills which they had practiced daily at Hunter Field. They played faithfully at all football games and pep meetings.

By 1958-1959 the Wilkinsburg High School Marching Band had grown to over one hundred members.

The 1950 basketball season opened with an attractive new addition to the squad - five girl cheerleaders, the first WHS has ever had. After a short training season, and an election, the girls were ready for the opening league season. Their uniforms consisted of blue skirts just below the knee with red pleats. They also had white pullover sweaters with tiger heads and small W's. White socks, saddle shoes, and red and blue beanies completed the ensemble. With this bright new attraction, attendance and cheering increased immensely.

Despite the hard work involved, competition for the few positions on the cheerleading squad was keen when the tryouts were held. As always, the WHS cheerleaders considered it a privilege to cheer our teams to victory. Two boys and five girls were on the 1955 squad. By 1956 only girls were on the squad and has remained that way. Over the years boys sometimes participate in leading cheers.

Friday pep meeting! As the curtain rose, the band in its bright red and blue uniforms began playing a lively Sousa march. These drummers were part of the 1952-1953 band.   Throughout the pep meetings it played school songs which were led by the cheerleaders. The most popular songs and cheers were published in the Student Handbook at the start of every school year.

SCHOOL SONGS

FOR YOU, HIGH

For you, high, for you, our gallant red and blue,
We always will support you, in everything you do,
We'll share all joy and gloom, whatever comes to
    you;
And we'll always win our games, for you, high.
For you high, we'll uphold your fame.

RED AND BLUE
By Jack Rodgers

Wilkinsburg High School, our Alma Mater,
Honor and loyalty we promise to you;
Your banner o'er us, leading on victorious,
Sing we the praises of the Red and Blue.
Here's to the colors of our dear high school,
Here's to our Alma Mater dear to each heart.
Here's to our honor and to our traditions;
So far for her glory we will do our part.
Hail Alma Mater! Guide for us always.
May all your sons and daughters ever be true,
Lighting our torches from the shrines of learning.
Building your standards in our lives for you.

VICTORY SONG

Come let's give a rousing cheer for High.
Cheer until our voices reach the sky. ,
A yell or two for Red and Blue.
Our songs we sing, let's make them ring
When the team is trying hard to win.
Everybody's shouting, "Don't give in."
Fight! Fight! Fight for High School,
Cheer the team to victory.

WILKINSBURG

Wilkinsburg, Wilkinsburg, to you we will be true,
We'll never be disloyal to our colors, Red and Blue.
Dear old High, dear old High, our love to you we'll
    prove;
And when we must part, we'll leave you our heart:
And we'll always remember you.

WHS was proud of its twelve high-stepping majorettes who strutted and twirled in front of the band in 1952-1953. The girls added color and entertainment to the pep meetings as well as to the half-time shows.

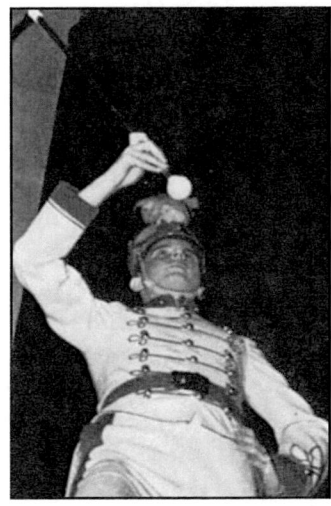  

Bob Travis, head drum major, did a wonderful job with his tremendous fast twirling and high tossing exhibitions in 1953.

Paul Staudt as drum major performed at a pep meeting in 1955.

Heading the majorette squad in 1953-55 was Pat Reno, the first junior at WHS to become head majorette. Her ability to gracefully twirl two batons simultaneously held the attention of all spectators.

WHS 1953-54 Marching Band

Wilkinsburg Tigers had a long-standing rivalry with Penn (Hills) Indians. Here the cheerleaders wore Indian headbands as they performed a skit during a pep meeting before a football game in 1956.

In 1956 a pep meeting at chapel excited the Tigers fans.

WHS students added another log to the wood pile at Turner Field. That wood pile became a blazing bonfire the night before the football victory over Penn in 1956. The tradition of a bonfire before Penn games continued for about a decade.

1954-1955 WHS Marching Band

The WHS band performed at all football games, Winter Concert, Spring Concert, and various community events. The Kiwanis Club Tri-State Marching Band Festival was first held in 1953 and became an annual event.

2nd ANNUAL

Tri-State Marching

Band Festival

Presented by

Kiwanis Club of Wilkinsburg

for the benefit of their

Underprivileged Child Work

Saturday, Sept. 11th

8:15 p.m.

GRAHAM FIELD - Wilkinsburg

Featuring

Massillon, Ohio High School Band

AND

WEIRTON, W. VA.	NEW KENSINGTON
ALIQUIPPA	CANONSBURG
BALDWIN TWP.	WILKINSBURG

RESERVED SECTION SEATS $1.50

Mail orders with remittance to

PFAFF'S PHARMACY

808 Penn Ave., Wilkinsburg 21, Pa.

General Admission $1.00   Advance Students 75¢

This flier in 1954 advertised the Band Festival
presented annually by the Kiwanis Club.

1957
WINTER
CONCERT

Wilkinsburg High School A Cappella Choir

Wilkinsburg High School Band

DR. WM. M. POTTER, Superintendent

EDWARD F. EGE, Principal

Thursday, February 7, 1957

8:15 P. M.

HIGH SCHOOL AUDITORIUM

Stage Crew, known as "the men behind the scenes", helped make WHS stage productions successful.

Stage Crew's duties, often unseen by the audience, are numerous and varied. Theirs is the job of raising and lowering the curtains at the proper times; the construction, painting, repairing and handling of all scenery; the moving of heavy stage properties; and the all-important sound-effects.

THE HI WAYS

Do Your Christmas Shopping Early

Roar! With The Tigers

WAYS, WINS & WIT OF WILKINSBURG HIGH SCHOOL

Vol. 35 No. 1   Wilkinsburg, Pa., High School   Wednesday, September 3, 1952

'Tiger Rag' Resounds As WHS Band Prepares Shows New Uniforms Added; Twelve Majorettes Perform

Wilkinsburg High's Tiger Band steps out in new uniforms this year as the sixty one guys and gals in the band, twelve majorettes and drum major, strut their stuff for another season. The sixty one includes eleven trumpets, four trombones, six saxs, fourteen clarinets, six horns, two baritones, three basses, flute, piccolo, seven drums, two bell lyres, and four color guard.

Current innovation of the band (in addition to new uniforms) is the increase in size of the majorette squad. Classes were held in junior high to train majorettes last spring. Veteran majorettes Sandy Bunt, Nora Ahn Reho, Marlene Curnow, and Sandra Miller, lead the majorettes in practices three times a week during the summer at Graham Field. Newly named majorettes are Mary Carden, Shirley Davis, Janet Gray, Ellen Carroll, Janice McGregor, Peggy Daw, Bobby Thompson, and Pat Reno.

Tempo Increases

Director Richard L. Camp announces the tentative plans of the Tiger Band, with Bob Travis as drum major, to present shows during grid half-

To The Rear, March

Tiger Band majorettes step through a practice session at Hunter Field, center, as band members go through drills, upper left and lower right. Drum Major Bob Travis looks things over, lower left, while Director Richard Camp prepares for work.

times which will include a Transportation Show, Rodeo, Old Time Square Dance, and a Salute to the Services. Director Camp, who has also led the bands of West View and Wilmerding High Schools, plans to increase the marching tempo, and introduce more precision work into the program of the band.

Mr. Camp plans to make us of five students from WJHS as band alternates, this year.

Ahead of Last Year

Twice-daily practice, both at Hunter Field and on stage, has been the band's diet during the past two weeks. Far in advance of last year, Director Camp explained Friday, August 22 at Hunter Field "We weren't doing this much at this time last year." The initial grid scrap was also a week earlier in September, last year.

Smith Student Leader

Band Student Director will be junior Bruce Smith, from the bass section. He will direct the band in the absence of Mr. Camp.

Officers will be elected by band members

(Continued on Page 2)

$10.00 Goes To Top Room For Selling Grid Tickets

$10.00 will be awarded to the homeroom whose members sell the most season adult reserved tickets to Tiger home football games, according to Mr. William P. Lohr, Athletic Administrator, in the period starting today and extending to Thursday, September 11, at the close of school. The winning room can divide the prize money among the students in the room any way they see fit. A second prize of $7.50, and a third prize of $5.00 are also being offered.

Sell for $6.00

Cost of the season ticket is $6.00, and they may be secured from Mr. Lohr.

Single game reserved tickets are not included in the contest.

Season Books On Sale

Student season books will be on sale next week, in the homerooms, at a price of $1.25. Single game student tickets sold at school the day of the game will be fifty cents.

As I See It
by Bob McKnight

Greetings:

As you can see, another new column has been added to The Hi-Ways. The purpose of this column is to give the staff's views of school developments. During the year our comments will be critical of some things and complimentary of others. Our opinion does not necessarily reflect that of the school or its students.

Unless you are a member of Wilkinsburg's infamous underground boys, you probably believe this has been Wilkinsburg's deadest summer. No Fourth of July celebration, no nothing! Of course, thanks to the Chamber of Commerce, there was the annual Community Picnic which was a great success.

WOW!!

Johnston school sure does look mighty nice after its session with the sand blaster. It looks kind of like a brand new school. Congrats to the School Board for beautifying our buildings.

That's a nice new floor you have in the cafeteria, Mrs. Fallon.

It seems that pigeons simply adore the Wilkinsburg School District. Graham Field and High School are simply loaded with the things. When you open a

Handbook Free

Student council's new free WHS student handbook, produced during the spring and summer by SC and former sponsor, Miss Helen Anderson, will be available today to all sophs, in the home rooms. Juniors and seniors interested in finding out where they've been these past few years may secure copies on request, also free of charge.

Greetin's

Eleven new students registered before Thursday, August 21 to come to WHS this year. They are: Arlene Zaharchak, Marlene Shturtz, Robert Lowe, from Edgewood; Jacqueline Day, Penn High; Isabell Dimon, from Peabody; Donald Sink, Mt. Lebanon; Patricia Wilachl, Sacred Heart;

New Profs Join Teaching Staff
by Ken Peters

Several of the faculty will not be back this year including Miss Edna Reitz and Miss Helen Anderson, both of whom retired at the end of school last year; Mrs. Harriet Naser who will be teaching commercial subjects at Penn High this year; Mrs. C. D. Jerrey, who taught girls' hygiene year and Mel Munsce hygiene instructor as basketball and driver's

New te Miss Do teach g Oetting The Englis Basho more

Mrs. Ege's Naser, and in the Dean John Kistler has been appointed to full time driver-training teacher as Miss Myrtle Wilson takes over as clothing instructor. Business manager for the Annual will be Miss Elizabeth Steele, and Miss Viola Smith will now have three senior classes of English and two of juniors. Miss Witherspoon will take over Miss Smith's duties as Jr.-Sr. Y-Teen sponsor. New boys' hygiene teacher will be Mr. S. Ray Grimm, grid coach.

Gum Gone

In addition to the changes in the administration, the school itself has undergone a series of changes. The boys' locker room has had a facelifting. A new floor of asphalt tile has been laid in the cafeteria, and all the gum has been removed from underneath the tables.

Stage Fixed In May, 1953; $35,000 Cost Double; Board Says "It Looks Bad."

Proposed and much-talked-about work on the WHS auditorium will be laid aside until next spring, according to Superintendent W. M. "We tried to get it in, but it would cost anticipated." The final decision was the board Thursday evening, August

the auditorium renovation at specifications were taken into to $35,000.

unit

Superintendent, the day following only after a lot of the last night, and it really things to be done. The

continued Dr. Potter, on the list of improvements were afraid that it might how, it would probably be regular chapel. It isn't only part, as everything must be renovated. The auditorium had part, as everything must be renovated. The auditorium has built.

Costs More at Johnston

"A couple of things we ran into cost more than we anticipated. The pointing work done on Johnston School was expected to run $14,000. By the time it was finished the cost was $19,500," the Superintendent stated.

"We've put more into the Senior High than we have into half of the other buildings," said Dr. Potter; "Future plans include completely rebuilding the showers in the boys lockers, and within two or three years, we will be modernizing several departments of the high school," he concluded.

Miss Long Named Sponsor

Miss Ruth Long is the sponsor of the student council this year, replacing Miss Helen Anderson.

Twenty-Four On S. C.

Student Council and representative assembly are the two student government organizations of WHS. Elections for student council are held in the fall and the spring and the members of the

elected each year by their respective classes. Suggestions and new projects originating in the student council are carried to the representative assembly which makes them known to the student, through each home room representative.

Operates Lost & Found

The Hi-Ways is the school newspaper, published during the year by the journalism class and the newspaper staff of Wilkinsburg High School. In addition to reporting news of events that took place within the school, the newspaper provided an anecdotal record of life at WHS and served as an outlet for student writing, art, and photography. *The Hi-Ways* held a first-place rating in all three of the national press associations: Columbia School Press Association, National Scholastic Press Association, and Quill and Scroll.

The Hi Ways publication started in 1931 following 25 years of the *Review*. It was truly 'The Home of Pride' at Wilkinsburg High School.

Wilkinsburg High School celebrated Christmas in a variety of ways.

Christmas in the 1950s and 1960s always included caroling in the halls by the A Cappella Choir, embellishing home room doors with a Christmas theme and Student Council members decorating a large tree in the front hall.

A Cappella choir caroled in the halls of WHS in 1954.

Band members led the choir for caroling in 1956.

Students in 1956 decorated class doors for Christmas.

Student Council decorated the school
Christmas tree in 1958.

The annual Christmas tree was decorated in 1960
by members of Student Council.

Chapel tradition ended after 50 years

Chapel was one of the many things that made Wilkinsburg High School superior. The Pledge of Allegiance led by the principal started every chapel meeting. In 1960 the pledge was led by Dr. Harry Pry.

Dr. Pry led the Pledge of Allegiance with the 1960 class officers.

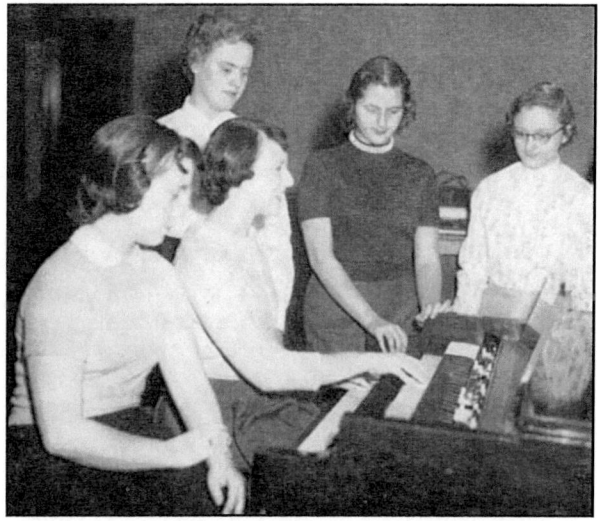

The music department provided talented student organists who were a vital part of daily chapel. These girls were the organists for the 1956-57 school year.

Chapel

It's not just "assembly" in Wilkinsburg High,
It's chapel - a pause in the day
When students and teachers sit down side by side,
And worries drift slowly away.

It's not just "assembly" in Wilkinsburg High,
It's something with roots in the past-
An honored tradition kept breathing and warm
By students who want it to last.

It's not just "assembly" in Wilkinsburg High,
It's music - The Bible - a prayer -
The choir's responses that come drifting down
With harmony sweet through the air.

It's not just "assembly" in Wilkinsburg High,
The seniors recall with a sigh;
They're leaving a spirit, a symbol, behind,
For chapel IS Wilkinsburg High.

Barbara Weeks, '47

Student Council member Nancy Glunt dismisses chapel.

Chapel at ten o'clock was the best-loved period in the daily routine of WHS. Students and faculty alike looked forward to this peaceful interlude of devotional exercises. The organ music played, then paused and a selected senior stepped to the podium where the Bible was. He or she read and was answered from the balcony by the blended voices of the A Cappella Choir. Frequently programs were planned to add entertainment featuring outstanding speakers, and an occasional "song" chapel. During the football season Friday programs were popular because of the pep meetings. After that an inspiring hymn, announcements, a tap of the gavel, and ...on to third period class.

In 1962 senior Jack Webster (pictured) took his turn to read the Bible in chapel. In June of 1962 the federal Supreme Court ruled that there could be no prayer or religion in public schools. Later that same year the government ruling ended WHS' daily tradition of chapel, one that had lasted for over 50 years.

The orchestra provided the best in music for the listening pleasure of WHS.

WHS would lack a great deal of spirit without the orchestra. These talented students furnish the music for our school plays, for our concerts, and for our music festivals. Orchestra members are often eligible to try-out for the state orchestra which provides unlimited possibilities for music study.

These student musicians were members of the 1954-1955 WHS orchestra.

This WHS orchestra was directed by Richard L. Camp in this 1966-1967 school year image.

Musicians contributed vocal talent to chapel and concerts

The WHS A Cappella Choir, was first organized in 1931 by Dr. Frank C. Biddle, and was made up of 50 seniors. It grew in popularity and soon had over sixty members whom Mr. Robert Barkley chose by private auditions based on voice quality, ability to read music, and cooperation. The WHS choir was a vital part of Wilkinsburg's Holy Week Services, Christmas and spring concerts and the daily chapel programs. Also each year it appeared before organizations, such as the Rotary, Kiwanis, and Women's clubs in Wilkinsburg and before churches, civic clubs, and meetings throughout the Pittsburgh area. It has also sung before the Annual National Safety Convention and The Western Pa Teacher's convention.

WHS 1950-51 A Cappella choir, directed by Mr. Robert O. Barkley

WHS Alumni often returned to sing with the A Cappella choir in Alumni chapel. This image shows choir participants in 1962 donning their robes.

A Cappella students had the leadership of Mr. Barkley who directed the choir from 1936 to 1963. This image shows Robert O. Barkley, Director of Music in 1943.

WHS band members practiced at band camp and performed for the community.

Band president Norm Hedding led cheers on the train to Greensburg in 1952.

Tiger horn players at band camp, 1960

Marching band performed at the 1962 Diamond Jubilee, celebrating 75 years of Wilkinsburg's incorporation.

Drummers at Camp Fairfield in 1960

Camp Fairfield in Ligonier held band camp every August for WHS Marching Tiger Band members. This image was taken in the mid 1950s.

There's music in the air! The social highlights each year were the WHS dances.

The first big dance of the year was held annually by the Varsity Club. The dance was promoted, advertised, arranged, and decorated for entirely by the boys themselves. Wilkinsburg High has always been proud of the Varsity Club, as its high standards and qualities are representative of a truly great organization.

Key Club in 1953 sponsored a dance "The Pigskin Parade," and a car wash. The money raised was donated toward the purchase of a plaque to honor the men and women from Wilkinsburg High School who served in World War II. Key Club was a credit to WHS and the community.

The 1956-57 Senior Counselors held a dance in honor of the exchange student from Holland, Tonny van der Hoeven.

In 1962 students hung streamers in the gym to decorate for the Junior Prom.

Ushers in 1955 were neatly attired in blue coats with bright red ties. It was the duty of these boys to insure the safety of the students in an emergency, keep a reasonable amount of quiet in chapel, help at the elections and seat audiences at all school performances. To be a member, boys needed petitions signed by four teachers and fifty students, and then voted on by Student Council. It was in 1960 that Student Council voted to include girls, thus the beginning of WHS usherettes. These young women were the first seven usherettes for WHS.

THE SPOON TRADITION

The school spoon is handed down each year by the graduating class to the succeeding Senior Class, to bestow upon them the responsibility of upholding and maintaining the school ideals. Each student should pledge himself to respect these ideals of loyalty, honor, leadership, and scholarship for the welfare of his school.

The spoon was first sponsored by the Class of 1901 to its successor and since that time the custom has become an annual occurrence. During the year it remains in a glass enclosed case in the library so that all may see and keep in mind the ideals it represents.

The WHS student handbook explained the spoon.

  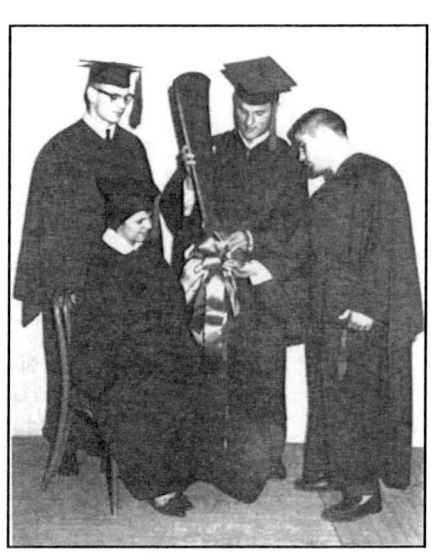

1955 class officers with the spoon   1963 class president   1960 class officers

WHS helped each student to develop a logical, well-disciplined mind.

Mr. Kenneth Tedrow taught math students to use a slide rule in this 1950 image.

Biology teacher Mr. Weigand reviewed entomology in 1950.

Miss Covil's math class

Chemistry students in 1950 worked with a lab partner on experiments.

Geometry and Trigonometry were offered to juniors and seniors.

Student Bill Wilson explains an interest problem to his economics class.

Student handbook contained a partial list of trophies WHS students had won.

1952 handbook list of trophies

TROPHIES

The following trophies won by Wilkinsburg High School are in the cases in the hall of the first floor of the old building. Most of them are for athletic supremacy.

1. Harvard Club Western Pa. Interstate Baseball _____ 1912
2. University of Pittsburgh—Western Pa. Championship Track Meet _____ 1913
3. W. P. I. A. L. Relay Championship, Schenley Oval _____ 1913
4. Westinghouse Club Interscholastic Indoor Track Meet _____ 1914
5. Syracuse Trophy for W. P. I. A. L. Football Championship _____ 1914
6. Smith Drug Co. Interscholastic Relay _____ 1914
7. W. P. I. A. L. Mile Relay _____ 1914
8. W. & J. Interscholastic Sports _____ 1914
9. Ross Hosack & Brothers Interscholastic Indoor Track _____ 1914
10. Rowland Theatre Dual Meet— Wilkinsburg vs. Shadyside _____ 1914
11. Syracuse Cup for W. P.. I. A. L. Football Championship _____ 1915
12. Literary Contest— Peabody vs. Wilkinsburg _____ 1916
13. W. P. I. A. L. Championship for Football _____ 1916
14. Syracuse Cup for W. P. I. A. L. Championship _____ 1916
15. Spalding Brothers Trophy for W. P. I. A. L. _____ 1917
16. Carnegie Tech Interscholastic Meet _____ 1917
17. W. P. I. A. L. Relay Championship _____ 1917
18. Volunteers of America Assistance rendered on Tag Day _____ 1919
19. Syracuse Cup for W. P. I. A. L. Football Championship _____ 1922
20.. University of Pittsburgh Cup _____ 1922
21. W. P. I. A. L. Basketball Championship _____ 1922

22. Pika Football Trophy— Wilkinsburg vs. Union _____ 1922
23. Football used in State Championship Game _____ 1922 (Wilkinsburg vs. Washington)
24. Point Trophy Pittsburgh Press Independent Track and Field Meet _____ 1922
25. Point Trophy Spalding Brothers East Borough Track Meet _____ 1925
26. Spalding Trophy for East Borough Track Meet _____ 1926
27. Pittsburgh Press Independent District Football _____ 1927
28. Pittsburgh Press Independent District Fooothall _____ 1927
29. Pittsburgh Press Boys' Trophy— Track and Field Meet _____ 1927 Pennsylvania Relay _____ 1927
30. Shady Side Academy Interscholastic Relay _____ 1928
31. Pittsburgh Press Track and Field Meet _____ 1928
32. Pittsburgh Press Independent High Schools Section 2 _____ 1928
33. Presented by Day Students _____ 1928
34. News Cup Triangular Track and Field Meet at New Castle _____ 1929
35. Pittsburgh Press Championship Trophy for Baseball _____ 1930
36. Warner Brothers' Rowland Theater for Greensburg Defeat _____ 1931
37. Warner Brothers to Football Team _____ 1932
38. Independent District Track and Field Meet _____ 1936
39. Marybill Cup Interclass Basketball _____ No Date
40. Simpson Pharmacy Trophy—Western
41. Murdock Ice Cream Co. Interclass Cup—
42. Pittsburgh High School vs. Wilkinsburg—Oratorical Contest _____ No Date
43. Independent District, Track and Field Meet, first place _____ 1937

44. Independent District, Relay Championship _____ 1937
45. Third Place Model Airplane Contest—Hunt Armory _____ 1937
46. Pittsburgh Fencers Club Third
47. Bob McKnight Award Wilkinsburg High
48. Fencing Champion Boys Team Western Pennsylvania _____ 1940
49. Fencing Champion Girls Team Western Pennsylvania _____ 1941
50. Mansfield Relays Two Mile Relay _____ 1941
51. Wilkinsburg Hi School Bowling League _____ 1940
52. —1945-47 Wilkinsburg Section VIII winners _____ 1947
53. —1947-48 Wilkinsburg Section VIII winners _____ 1948
54. W. P. I. A. L. Track Championship _____ 1948
55. 2nd Place Indoor Tri State Championship _____ 1951
56. W. P. I. A. L. Mile Relay Trophy _____ 1951
57. Section XV Baseball Trophy _____ 1951

Wilkinsburg High School published and distributed a student handbook at the beginning of each school year. It contained information of interest to the students. This copy in 1952 included a list, though not complete, of the trophies in the WHS trophy case and gave the students an idea of the athletic supremacy of those who had attended WHS.

WHS had an undefeated season due to the hard work of the 1950-51 Cross Country team in its third season. This "young" team came through its seven meets victoriously; then took second place in WPIAL and fourth in State Championships at State College. Star "point-getters" were Al Myers, Chuck Fritz, Marty Ide, Al Frederick, Bob Weals, and Jim Flynn. Future prospects are bright as the Junior Varsity team was also undefeated and finished fourth in the WPIAL meet.

This 1953 baseball team was put in perfect condition by Coach William Lohr. The boys practiced in the gym until the weather permitted them to practice outside at Turner Field. The team finished the season with 7 wins and 3 losses - a second place in their section.

In June '53 two boys, Barry Fullerton and Charles Cost represented WHS at Forbes Field in the All-Star game.

Wilkinsburg's 1953 track season reached a sterling climax in the annual WPIAL championship meet at Connellsville.

The Tiger trackmen topped Mt. Lebanon and a field of twenty-three other high school track squads from seven Western Pennsylvania counties to win the WPIAL track and field meet with a total of 27 1/2 points.

The WPIAL meet was a qualifier for the statewide PIAA competition a week later at State College, PA. The mile relay team of Larry Brunner, Ed Hartman, Leonard Kaiser, Ken Dredel went on to become the state mile relay champions in the PIAA meet.

This WHS track team included state mile-relay champions!

WHS's 1955 track team upheld the high expectations of their coach, Mr. John Browning (first row, far right). The Browning-men won all - six out of six - of their dual meets. They also toppled some WHS records: Ed Hartman ran the 1/4 mile in 51.1 seconds; Joe Harvey threw the discus 142'11"; Larry Brunner ran the mile in 4'32.7; the mile relay team, former state champions, broke their previous year's time by running the mile in 3'30.7; and the sprint medley relay team - Ed Hartman, Dave Wright, Bill Guhl, and Larry Brunner - broke the indoor record with 4'48.8. The team compiled more first places than any other team in the WPIAL.

In 1955, having the finest basketball team in five years, Coach Walt Miller turned them into winners in regular season play with seventeen wins and five losses. The starting lineup included: Steve Filipowski, Rich Branzel, Ron Shadd, Dick Cain, Bill Sapp, Dan Gearhart, and Wes McElroy. Tied with Penn for first place, the Tigers met the Indians at Pitt Stadium for the WPIAL Section VII Play-off. Sparked by Rich Branzel and Steve Filipowski, the Tigers slaughtered Penn by the score of 52-37.

Wrestling was added in 1955 to the list of varsity sports. Predictions are that with experience the wrestling team will be one of the strongest in the state.

1957 triumphant Tigers end grid schedule with WPIAL championship!

The 1957 WHS football team , under Coach Clarke Miller, started the season by defeating city league foes, Allderdice 19-7 and Peabody 34-0. Then the league competition loomed ahead in Greensburg, the first WPIAL opponent. It was trounced by WHS 25-6. Then Latrobe was beaten 13-7. After Trinity fell before the surging gridders, thoughts of the Foothills trophy came into fans' minds. When WHS scored a triumphant victory over Mt. Lebanon 24-6, local and city papers began recounting the exploits of the Millermen. October 26 was the date of the game with undefeated, untied Hempfield Area High. A last period rally, which pulled the Tigers through to another victory, 20-18, proved the value of teamwork and many hours of practice. With the win over Jeannette, 40-7, the Foothills championship was clinched. The Penn Indians, arch rivals, presented a problem in a driving rain, but they were defeated 6-0 to assure Wilkinsburg High of an undefeated season. Then came the agonizing wait to hear the outcome of the Jeannette-Connellsville game which determined who would play in the WPIAL championship game. The result was a meeting with Clairton at Pitt Stadium November 30. On that snowy afternoon the underdog Tigers surprised the Bears with a smashing 13-0 victory. Cheers, blowing horns, and excited yells resounded in the Holy City that evening when the victorious team returned after winning the first trophy since 1922. A festive banquet at the Holiday House in Monroeville climaxed one of the greatest football seasons in this area in many years.

WHS students admire the WPIAL and Foothills Conference trophies before they are placed in the trophy case in 1957.

The WHS trophy cases were filled with proof of student athletic ability over the years. This image is from 1962.

WHS' baseball team became repeat WPIAL section champions!

Diamond lettermen compiled a favorable record in 1958. Under the capable coaching of Mr. William Parkinson the WHS baseball team reigned in first place in their WPIAL section for the second consecutive year. Their record for the two years included seventeen wins and two defeats in section play. With five wins and one loss behind them, WHS entered their games with Penn. After these games Wilkinsburg emerged with a 9-1 record and a first-place position. In WPIAL play-offs, the team recorded victories over Trafford, 9-3 and favored Brownsville, 7-3. WHS played the final game with Freeport, who won, thereby giving Freeport the championship.

1961 WHS basketball team captured the WPIAL section championship. Coach Walter Miller's court-men posted a 23-3 record and went to the quarter-finals of the WPIAL Class A tourney. The Tigers defeated Mt. Lebanon, Norwin, Stowe, Arnold, Langley and Greensburg. The Tigers, participating in the Ford City Kiwanis Tournament, beat Dayton and Ford City to bring the championship trophy home. The Tiger team ended its exhibition schedule at 9-1 after pounding Latrobe, 61-33.

1961 wrestlers won three dual meets and placed third in Section 2 competition with 17 points. Rick Wortman, Tom Grim and Jack Banks battled their way to the final round in WPIAL competition but did not go further. Jack White (second from the right in this "W" formation) qualified for regional competition and won the second WPIAL championship for WHS by defeating Radosovich of German Township, 5-4, in the finals of the 180-pound class.

The 1960-1961 wrestlers qualified for regional competition.

Wilkinsburg was the basketball section winner in 1963. The Tiger Team was led by Daniel (Dan) Kane and Norris (Happy) Clark. They beat Turtle Creek in the section playoff and in the quarter-final they beat Butler. In the semi-final the team lost to Norwin.

Tigers claim the Foothills Conference Title

In 1961, for the second time in five years Head Coach Clarke T. Miller guided the Wilkinsburg Tigers to the WPIAL Class AA playoff game. The Tigers opened the 1961 season with a 47-0 victory at Graham Field against Taylor Alderdice. The Tigers finished their schedule undefeated. The last regular season game was against arch rival Penn Hills. The Tiger victory (9-6 over the Indians) was witnessed by over 10,000 fans, and gave WHS a maximum total of 150 Gardiner points and a berth in the WPIAL Championship playoff game. The valiant Wilkinsburg Tigers lost a heart-breaking 7-6 battle at Forbes Field to the highly rated Monessen Hounds for the WPIAL Class AA championship.

The 1961 Tigers did win the Foothills Conference Title. In 1961 Mr. Abraham, (third from the left) President of the Foothills Conference, presented the trophy to Mr. Bill Lohr, Mr. Clarke Miller, and Mr. Walter Miller. . Our hats are off to the WHS coaches for making our colors, Red and Blue, stand high in the field of sportsmanship.

In 1967 John Mackay and Larry Hurt wore their new Tiger-embellished uniforms as they listened to the advice of basketball coach James E. Wilkinson.

1963 tennis team captured Section 5 Title - Coached by Mr. Master, the section 5 tennis championship went to WHS, with a record of 11-1. The Tigers' home court was Ferguson Playground.

Rugged determination defined the 1968 Tigers' season.

Grid-iron action showed the determination of the hard-hitting 1968 Tigers. The team travelled to North Allegheny to meet their first double-A opponents. After an easy victory over NA, the next game was against Jeannette. Wilkinsburg remained on the winning track with a score of WHS-32 to Jeannette-6.

The Tigers hosted their next opponents, the Greensburg Lions, in what became the most spectacular game of the season. The score during the first half of the game kept team morale low. A rousing pep-talk at the half provided the necessary boost for winning the game. This suspenseful game was won by the WHS Tigers with only thirty-five seconds remaining in the game. The final score was WHS-51 to Greensburg-50. Next, Wilkinsburg emerged victorious against the undefeated Latrobe Wildcats. The next victory was against the Norwin Knights in Wilkinsburg's highest scoring game of the season, (WHS-53 to Norwin-12). After losses to Connellsville and Hempfield, WHS held Kiski scoreless in a 14-0 game. For the final game of the season, WHS held rival Penn Hills scoreless in a 13-0 game.

With an admirable record of seven wins and two losses the Tigers completed the 1968 season. Because of the determined effort of the team, this was one of the foremost seasons in Wilkinsburg's football history.

Pep talk at half time gave the Tigers a winning boost in the Greensburg game. The final score in that game was WHS-51 to Greensburg-50.

WHS cheerleaders welcome the Tigers at the beginning of the Norwin game.. The final score in that game was WHS-53 to Norwin-12.

In 1962, WHS had two national champions in the student body.

Andi Hopkins was the 1962 National Women's 250-Yard Breaststroke Champion (time 3:15.2)

Marty Sixsmith, our national twirling champion highlighted WHS games and pep rallies with her flashy twirling routines.

Lettermen highlighted the year with the annual varsity dance, planned and carried out entirely by Varsity Club members. In 1960 (left to right) Varsity Ball queen Nancy Davis poses with attendants Fran Colonello and Barbara Garland accompanied by Varsity Club members Ed Snyder, Dan Connors, and Dwain Irvin.

WHS celebrated the Pittsburgh Pirates' win in the 1960 World Series. These senior girls performed a "Beat 'Em Bucs" song and skit.

WHS did not have varsity sports for girls in the 1960s. However, there was Leaders Club, a well-run intramural program, organized in 1932. The sports available were tennis, swimming, basketball, and volleyball. Girls in LC refereed games to earn points towards a letter. Points were also gained by timing, scoring and playing, and by selling programs at Graham Field during football season. A Leader needed to earn twenty

points a semester to retain her membership. When a girl earned 250 points, she had the honor of wearing a Red and Blue 'W'.

1962-1963 Leaders Club members were sports-minded girls who earned their emblems.

WHS majorettes practiced precision performances.

The Majorettes and Drum Majors put extra spark in the Wilkinsburg High pep rallies and Graham Field half-time performances, inspiring their team on to many victories. Under the leadership of Mary Ann Rocco, head majorette, and Mary Lee Scherm, assistant head, the girls practiced many hours at band camp and during the summer at "Little Graham Field".

The 1964 Majorettes performed well under the direction of Miss Joyce A. Weidman. They are (left to right) Janet Buch, Mary Lee Scherm, Maryann Rocco and Paulette Baranette.

In 1967, the Twirling Tigerettes were practicing daily under the direction of Head Majorette, Rosemary Hoffman.

Throughout the year, the Twirling Tigerettes performed at home and away games, pep rallies, and at a number of Band Festivals and parades.

Graham Field brings back memories to Wilkinsburg High School players and fans.

Graham Field, developed in 1916, has been the central place for athletics in Wilkinsburg for almost a century.

GRAHAM FIELD

Wilkinsburg High School students have available one of the best equipped athletic fields in the state, known as Graham Field. There is a new entrance at the upper part of the field in place of the tennis courts. The seating capacity now is nearly 7,000. Wilkinsburg has taken a step toward modern football by installing six steel towers with 18 lights on a tower and 54 lights on each side of the field.

Above information was taken from the 1952 Student Handbook.

The WILKINSBURG name was quite prominent in this 1964 image.

Graham Field brings back memories for Wilkinsburg High School alumni.

Wilkinsburg High School Commencement exercises were moved to Graham Field in 1931, because the grandstand provided increased seating for the large number of graduates. These images show students donning their caps and gowns prior to the ceremony, marching in pairs toward the grandstand, filing through the archway to their seats, and sitting for the speeches just before receiving diplomas. These photo images were all from the 1950s and 1960s.

**The size of a WHS diploma shrank over the years,
but its significance grew to those who had earned one.**

In 1915 the diploma measured 16 by 22 inches. In this 1952 image the diploma was slightly smaller. By 1956 it measured a mere 8 by 10 inches. No matter the size of the paper, a diploma from Wilkinsburg High School was valuable and many colleges and universities required no further evidence of high school education to be accepted for enrollment.

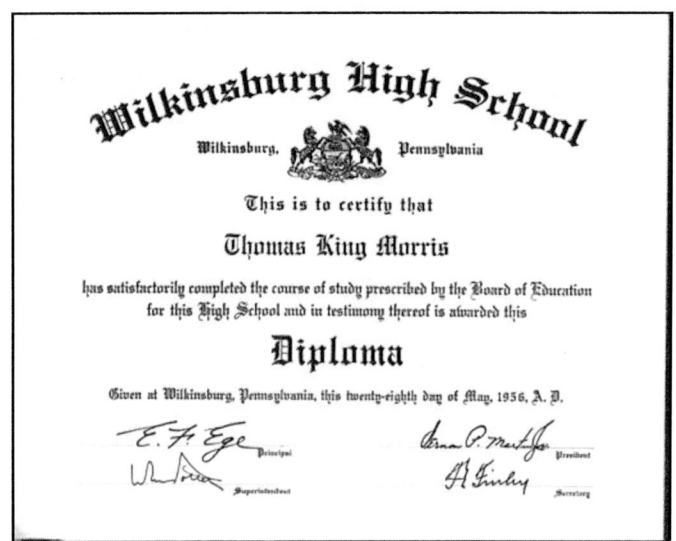

In 1956 a WHS diploma was presented as an 8 x 10 inch rolled-up document, tied with a red and blue ribbon.

In 1961 WHS changed to the folder-type diplomas.

To be a member of National Honor Society is both a privilege and an honor for a student of WHS. Each member must show not only scholastic aptitude but character, leadership, and service before he or she is entitled to wear the small gold emblem of this national organization. The gold pin is in the shape of a keystone with a flaming torch surrounded by four letters S.S.L.C. which signify the society's requirements. The National Honor Society insignia is also affixed to the diplomas of those who earned them.

In 1962 an interesting page of school facts was in the local newspaper.

Review Of School Officials; Senior Classes

WILKINSBURG PUBLIC SCHOOLS
Service of Personnel — Educational Administration

Superintendents:

J. D. Anderson	1877-1898
E. J. Shives	1898-1902
James L. Allison	1902-1922
William H. Martin	1922-December 1928
William C. Graham	January 1929-1941
R. A. Getter	1941-1950
William M. Potter	1950-1962

Principals:

Horner Elementary (-1927) Allison Elementary (1927-1962)

Mary H. Gibson	-1928
Millie S. Duff	1928-1932
Nelle P. Maxwell ·	1932-1948
Gladys P. Cannon	1948-1962

Johnston Elementary

Elizabeth O. Evans	1907-1927
· Marion R. Craig	1927-1953
Virginia R. Johns	1953-1962

Kelly Elementary

Anna M. Millar	-1915
Eleanor B. Ralston	1915-1926
Ella M. Brubaker	1926-1943
Clara M. Kirschner	1943-1949
Rilla M. Sterling	1949-1952
Harold B. Grim	1952-1962

McNair Elementary

Mary Bishop	-1910
Eleanor B. Ralston	1910-1915
W. Ray Smith	1915-1917
E. E. Hicks	1917-January 1918
Mary A. Gregg	February 1918-1928
Gertrude L. Fowles	1928-1944
Rilla M. Sterling	1944-1949 (School closed)

Semple Elementary

Floda McComb	-1915
Ira A. Black	1915-1917
Elizabeth J. Sloane	1917-1934
Mary E. Beatty	1934-1955
John M. Lowry	1955-1962

Turner Elementary

Edna P. Payne	1927-1952 (Supv. Teacher 1927-28)
Harry F. McKee	1952-1955
Sara Jane Van Ryn	1955-1962

Principals, Assistant Principals, Deans, Counselors:

Junior High School

E. E. Hicks	Principal	Feb. 1918-1928
Robert E. Beaton	Principal	1928-1942
Lucy E. Fiscus	Assistant Principal	1929-1930
Edward F. Ege	Student Counselor (Senior High also)	1929-1941
Howard M. Harper	Assistant Principal	1930-Jan. 1939
Elizabeth Clugston	Advisor to Girls	1930-1936
La Roux R. Allison	Advisor to Girls	1936-1946
La Roux R. Allison	Dean of Girls	1946-1957
Karl W. Bohren	Assistant Principal	Jan. 1939-1942
Karl W. Bohren	Principal	1942-1947
J. Glenn Smith	Principal	1947-1962
Thomas M. Phipps	Director of Activities	1952-1960
Evelyn H. Cable	Dean of Girls	1957-1959

Evelyn H. Cable	Dean of Girls — Guidance Counselor	1959-1962
Robert A. Hope, Jr.	Dean of Boys — Guidance Cunselor	1960-1962

Senior High School

W. P. Spargrove	Principal	1900-1903
William C. Graham	Principal	1903-Dec. 1928
F. H. Carson	Principal	Jan. 1929-1950 (U.S. Service 1942-1946)
R. A. Getter	Assistant Principal	1929-1941
Edna M. Reitz	Advisor to Girls	1929-1946
Edna M. Reitz	Dean of Girls	1946-1952
Edward F. Ege	Student Counselor (Junior High also)	1929-1941
Edward F. Ege	Assistant Principal	1941-1942
Edward F. Ege	Acting Principal	1942-1946
Edward F. Ege	Guidance Counselor	1946-1950
Edward F. Ege	Principal	1950-1962
Ernest J. Bishop	Guidance Counselor	1950-1962
G. Mothersbaugh	Dean of Girls	1952-1959
G. Mothersbaugh	Dean of Girls — Guidance Counselor	1959-1962
Wm. R. Parkinson	Dean of Boys	1958-1959
Wm. R. Parkinson	Dean of Boys — Guidance Counselor	1959-1962
Harry C. Pry	Principal	1959-1961
William P. Lohr, Jr.	Assistant Principal	1960-1961
William P. Lohr, Jr.	Principal	1961-1962

Membership of Graduating Classes

Year	No.	Year	No.	Year	No.
1887	3	1913	77	1940	478
1888	7	1914	99	1941	406
1889	10	1915	86	1942	420
1890	12	1916	62	1943	400
1891	10	1917	116	1944	350
1892	4	1918	89	1945	350
1893	10	1919	115	1946	350
1894	13	1920	148	1947	362
1895	15	1921	164	1948	384
1896	29	1922	173	1949	329
1897	1	1923	223	1950	316
1898		1924	254	1951	300
1899		1925	212	1952	310
1900	9	1926	273	1953	300
1901	14	1927	42/214=256	1954	290
1902	15	1928	48/205=253	1955	297
1903	25	1929	65/215=280	1966	347
1904	22	1930	70/235=305	1957	283
1905	32 (last 3-yr. class)	1931	67/206=273	1958	325
1906	None	1932	83/270=353	1959	350
1907	34 (first 4-yr. class)	1933	107/318=452	1960	435
1908	31	1934	480	1961	393
1909	36	1935	500	1962	342*
1910	71	1936	573		
1911	50	1937	460		
1912	83	1938	562		
		1939	443		

*22 additional registered for summer school who expect to receive diplomas.

Note: From 1927 through 1933 there were two graduating classes, in January and in May.

Cautious and efficient drivers were the product of the WHS Driver Education Department.

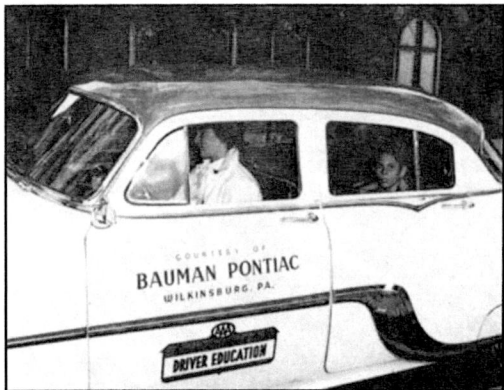 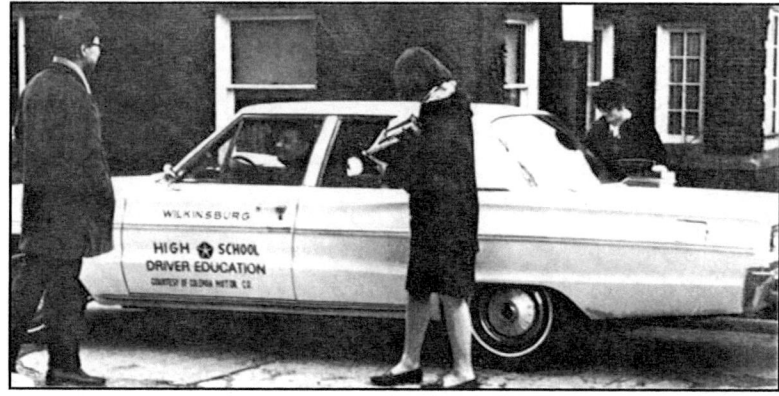

The driver training program in the 1950s and 60s was directed by Mr. Eugene Rotonto. After classroom theory in driver education, the students learned to drive in the presence of other students as well as their instructor. Driver Education taught many WHS students to become more considerate, responsible drivers.

The Department taught safety rules and highway regulations. Both classroom and behind-the-wheel instruction helped familiarize students with driving hazards and showed them how to cope with these problems. This classroom photograph shows Mr. Robert C. Matsey teaching in 1967.

Intellectual Tigers tackled math and science

In its diversified program Wilkinsburg High School recognizes the capabilities and interests of all Tigers as it tries to provide for everyone. Here are the Intellectual Tigers, tackling algebra, chemistry and physics problems in the early 1960s.

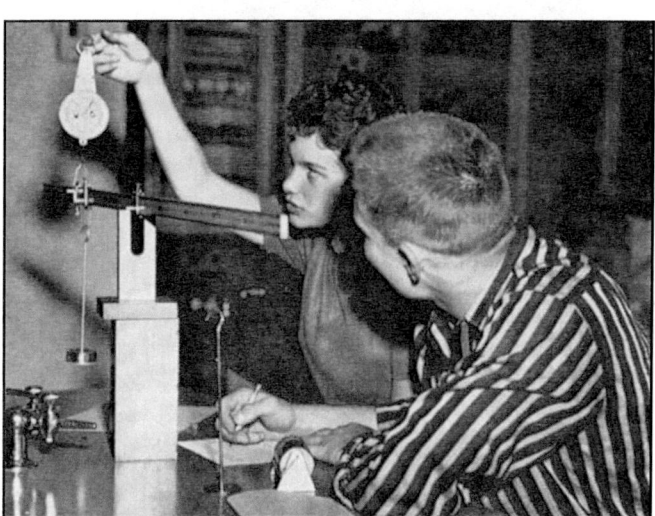

By the end of the 1960s Wilkinsburg High School was ready for a new cafeteria. These images show the old cafeteria which needed to be enlarged and updated for students of the 1970s.

1942-1943

1948-1949

As the 1960s ended, the high school and the Horner Middle School were scheduled to consolidate. Although improvements had been made in the cafeteria facility over the years, the school was in need of a much larger and more modern cafeteria to efficiently take care of the nutritional needs of the students. The School Board voted to build a cafeteria addition, and that was the first major accomplishment of the new decade.

1955 Lunch - The favorite period of the day for some students.

In 1956 some students "brown-bagged" their lunch. Note that milk was served in small glass bottles at that time.

Chapter 6 - Cafeterias, Computers and Clubs - 1970-1989

The enrollment figures which had spiralled upward during the 30s, 40s and 50s appeared to have reached a virtual plateau where they remained for the next four decades. The community had grown to its boundaries while rapid growth was just beginning in the rural suburban areas to the east. New school districts and high schools were being established in the rural suburban areas and students living in those areas would eventually leave the Wilkinsburg Schools.

The decades of the sixties and seventies were to a certain extent turbulent to both the community and society in general. Surrounded by disturbing historic events such as the Vietnam War, the assassinations of President John F. Kennedy, his brother Robert, and Martin Luther King Jr., the eventual resignation of President Richard Nixon, and the effects of the Energy Crisis, the schools entered an era of change. Students were actively involved in Vietnam War issues and in circumstances involving Civil Rights. Some of the elementary schools in the district had become racially segregated due to housing patterns which caused great concern within the community.

As the sixties ended, the district completed its most aggressive building program in over forty years. Kelly School was replaced by a modern air-conditioned building. Wilkinsburg High School was involved in an extensive remodeling project which included an addition to house a cafeteria. At Turner School plans were underway for a gymnasium-cafeteria addition, which was ultimately completed in the mid-seventies.

In 1971 the entire district underwent reorganization for the purpose of ending segregation. The attendance areas for all elementary schools were modified and Semple School was closed. All elementary schools were changed from K-6 to K-5. The junior high became Horner Middle School, serving students in grades 6-8. The high school served students in grades 9-12. Curricula in all schools were modified to serve a changing population in an era of rapid technological change. Specialized "mini-courses" were added to the traditional course offerings at the high school. The entire operation of the middle school was modified to reflect new trends in education. The elementary schools offered the option of the "open classroom" or "traditional classroom".

WHS as it appeared after the addition of the new cafeteria in 1969.
The cafeteria was constructed between the high school and the Baptist Church.

The cafeteria addition, constructed in 1969, was ready for WHS students of the 70s.

As the decade of the 1970s came to a close, the trends in education were changing toward a more traditional approach, or "back to basics". The district responded with another reorganization, which by 1981 ended with Allison School permanently closed, the high school returned to more traditional courses, the junior high school returned to a 7-9 format, and the sixth graders returned to the elementary schools. The "baby boom" had totally passed through the schools, and the district found itself with an excess of both classrooms and teachers. Compounding the problem was the fact that energy costs had spiraled upward during the previous decade increasing the total cost of education. In 1985 the Horner Junior High School was closed and Wilkinsburg Junior-Senior High School was created serving students in grades 7-12.

A student observes a workman on the scaffolding during construction of the new cafeteria in 1969.

Cafeteria construction was underway in this 1969 view looking toward Wallace Avenue.

The cafeteria women and the students enjoyed the large, bright and thoroughly modern cafeteria addition in 1970.

WHS students brought hearty appetites to the new cafeteria line

A great assortment of tasty food was available in the new cafeteria.

Gleaming stainless steel made sanitizing easy for the cafeteria staff.

Lunch time was also a social time for many of the students.

In 1971 students "fueled up" for their afternoon classes.

Students had a chance to eat, study, and sometimes get in a quick game of chess.

WHS helped students to feel comfortable using computers.

In the 1970s WHS entered the computer age with what was then a state-of-the-art IBM computer.

Students with computer skills are more valuable when it comes time to apply for jobs so WHS was one of the first schools in Allegheny County to offer a computer programming class for students. In the 1970s we had only one computer in each building. By the mid 1980s we had more than 100 computers in the Wilkinsburg Schools. There are numerous computer programs at Wilkinsburg High School designed to help students learn, including programs to help prepare for college board examinations.

In 1974 students are adding fan-fold, pin-fed paper to the computer.

In 1981-82 additional computers in the school meant that all students had a chance to use the new technology.

Students in computer class learned how to work with the new technology.

As WHS students became more proficient in computer use, additional classes were available for advanced study. These images were all taken in the 1970s and 1980s.

Computers continue to play an important role in student learning, especially in the areas of study skills and career planning.

In 1970 the library was modernized, enlarged, and air-conditioned.

The library was a tremendous asset to WHS. Carrels with tapes and film strips for individual viewing, a microfilm reader, and an audio-tutor aided students in their study. These, together with new rooms for seminars and conferences, made a very modern study center.

The school library had been upgraded with new lighting, air conditioning and seating that could be easily rearranged when necessary.

The well-lit library had originally been the 1911 auditorium. The curved, decorative ceiling had been the lower part of the 1911 balcony. In 1976 Principal Vernon Tipton conducted a faculty meeting.

In the early 1970s the school library was a bright, comfortable place to study. It was also used when the School Board held meetings which the public could attend. This view was in 1971 as Board members listened to citizen input.

Language lab and foreign language clubs were popular at WHS.

In the Foreign Language Department students used the Aural-oral method in their French, Spanish, and German classes to develop speech patterns and conversational skills. By reading and by seeing films, students learned the cultures of other countries.

The Foreign Language Department taught students to understand, to read, to speak, and to write foreign languages. To reach their goal, these students in 1970 made extensive use of the language lab.

In 1970 these German Club members could easily converse in German, due to their language lab training.

Chess Club encouraged its members to develop skills in the art of playing chess.

Chess Club at WHS originally started in 1920 with the aim to create interest in this scientific game. The club members met weekly to practice and hopefully become masters of the game. The WHS Chess Team was made up of the tournament winners from the club. The WHS Chess Team belonged to the Eastern Division of the Pittsburgh Chess League, one of the most competitive divisions in the area.

The best chess players in Chess Club became members of the WHS Chess Team. The Team, comprised of the five top players, gained the honor of participating in interscholastic competition with such opponents as Churchill, Penn Hills, St. Anselm, McKeesport, Swissvale, and Edgewood.

This image shows members of the 1969-70 Chess team.

Chess Club opened with a rugged elimination tournament. These are members of the 1979-80 Chess Club who met every week during the school year. Membership for the Chess Team was determined by a play-off tournament conducted in the spring with individual championship contests.

1978-79 Chess Club members

1988-89 Chess Club members

WHS taught students to drive and how to maintain and repair a vehicle.

One of the most practical courses offered students at WHS was the Driver Education course. Students learned the safe operation of motor vehicles, basic maneuvers and techniques necessary in everyday driving. Mr. Eugene Rotonto in vehicles and Mr. Robert Matsey in the classroom made a great team for teaching safe driving. These views are in 1971.

Boys in auto shop learned about automobile engine repair as well as motorcycle repair.

School spirit and Tiger pride!

The cheerleaders and majorettes worked diligently to promote school spirit, support the athletic teams, and uphold the name and standards of WHS. These dedicated girls created many new routines, cheers and chants to add to the WHS repertoire.

1970 majorettes

In 1972, WHS cheerleaders helped to excite the fans.

1977 squad

The WHS Cheerleaders worked throughout the year to promote Tiger pride. The squad led cheers at football games, basketball games, wrestling matches, and pep rallies. As part of their preparation for this work, the cheerleaders attended cheerleading camp at Robert Morris College where the squad often won ribbons for superior performance.

1972 squad at the school

By the late 1980s the cheerleading squad had increased to fifteen members. This image was taken in autumn of 1988.

Wilkinsburg Tiger Band played a big role in providing school spirit for Wilkinsburg High.

The band performed at football games, band festivals and parades in the area,
winning numerous performance awards for their talent and precision marching.

1971-72 Wilkinsburg High School Marching Band

1975 color guard

WHS 1971-72 Tiger Band members participated in festivals at Beaver Valley and East Allegheny and hosted the Kiwanis Band Festival at Graham Field. The band was also invited to march in a parade in Winchester, Virginia, during April.

Drum Major led the band at Graham Field.

Exuberance!

1975 Drum major Burt Lugar with assistant Jean Elliott.

1972 Cymbal player

The WHS Marching Tiger Band looked great COMING and GOING!

The 110 member Tiger Marching Band of 1977-78, under the direction of Mr. William Balawajder, performed at community and school events. Proudly wearing new uniforms, the band members entertained the crowds with pre-game and halftime shows at football games, hosted the Kiwanis Band Festival, and played for the Arts and Crafts Festival and Community Day. The band members also entertained at the annual Winter Concert as well as the Spring Festival. The highlight of the year was a trip to Disney World in Florida where the members of the band marched, representing WHS with pride.

Well-trained, reliable, colorful, and thrilling, the WHS Band was a special part of our school and community. At football games and pep rallies, its marches and songs contributed to our enthusiasm; in our parades it won many prizes for precision and ability; and in our hearts its music has become associated with the happiest and most memorable days of high school life.

WHS musical programs were highly regarded in the school and in the community.

Student organists were an important part of the assembly programs. These talented students took turns playing to enhance the programs. This group of WHS organists were photographed in 1972.

The saxophone players in the High School Band practiced almost daily under the skilled direction of Mr. Balawajder in this 1982 image.

1986 Dance Line members

In 1988 WHS featured a Dance Line, A Squad, Color Guard and a new name for the Tiger Marching Band, the "Aristocats", a variation of their wild Tiger theme.

The 1970s featured instrumental music groups under the direction of Mr. Ted Robins.

Several students were selected in 1970 for District Band. Those talented students were Dennis Parrish, Jeanine Varuola, Oliver Ragsdale and Don Varuola.

Stage Band of 1977-78

Stage Band was composed of members of the Tiger Marching Band. This band was a group of musicians who specialized in popular music. They began the year by performing for parents and friends at band camp. During the year they appeared at several concerts in school and in the community.

The instrumentation consisted of saxophones, trumpets, trombones, a French horn, a bass, piano, guitars, and drums. The Stage Band performed at pep rallies, Open House, and the music department's winter and spring concerts. This group, directed by Mr. Bill Balawajder, also hosted a clinic sponsored by the United States Navy Jazz Ensemble and an assembly concert by the Boyce Campus Jazz Gospel Choir.

WHS students filled the air with the sounds of beautiful vocal music.

The vocal music program provided students the opportunity to perform in large ensembles, small groups, and as soloists. The A Cappella Choir is a class, a club, and a performing group. Performances for the year included the Christmas Concert, Winter Band Concert, and Spring Music Festival. This A Cappella choir, under the direction of Mrs. Louise Lugar, posed in front of the school in 1981.

Madrigal Singers, Girls' Choir, Girls' Ensemble, Grace Notes, and Male Choir, were other vocal groups where the gifted students of WHS could share their talents. These are the Madrigal Singers in the early 1980s.

A Cappella Choir marched in the Community Day parade, October, 1988.

Wilkinsburg track teams have consistently shown amazing talent!

The 1970 track team had four members - Terry Jackson, John DeLeonardis, Steve Tucker, and Keith Hood - who became district qualifiers. John DeLeonardis was the lone Burg survivor in the state finals at Penn State. (Picture shows Steve Tucker, John DeLeonardis, and Paul Morris)

1971-72 track team showed a great deal of individual talent. Representatives of the team participated in many tournaments and frequently took first and second place. Terry Jackson took 1st place in the long jump at the Tri-State Outdoor meet, then 1st place in Connellsville at the Triangular Meet, 1st place in long jump at the WPIAL at Washington, and 1st place in long jump at the PIAA at Penn State to become the State Champion. Here is Terry Jackson in his championship form.

Terry Jackson flies while displaying championship form.

In 1972 the WHS track team competed in many local events and had a number of consecutive victories.

These 1970 track athletes easily cleared the hurdles.

WHS continued to develop athletic champions.

The 1988 Cross Country team had another successful season under Coach Thomas Rostek. The team posted a 4-4 record and only lost one home match. Rostek served as Cross Country coach for seventeen years, from 1978 to 1995.

Cross Country Champion Eric Downer is recognized by Coach Thomas Rostek.

In 1988 runner Eric Downer finished in first place in all home matches and set a course record of 15:57 for Wilkinsburg's difficult 3.1 mile Frick Park course. Eric went on to become Wilkinsburg's first WPIAL Cross Country Champion and placed second (by a mere 5 seconds) at the state finals.

William Brown, in 1989 won the WPIAL Class AA 110-meter high hurdles championship at Shippensburg University. He also qualified for the PIAA Championships in the long jump. Under Coach Rostek, Brown developed superb athletic ability.

Congratulations to the WPIAL Section VII Championship Team!

In 1975-76 WHS had a section-winning team for the first time since 1963. The championship brought joy to our students and fostered school spirit at WHS. The 1975-1976 Varsity Basketball Team was a source of pride to WHS. The men worked exceptionally hard, and the season's record reflected their efforts.

Again, Congratulations to the WPIAL Section VII Championship Team!

The year 1976-77 was difficult for the defending Section VII Champion Tigers. Every opponent keyed its hopes upon upsetting the defending champs who continued to represent WHS with pride, respect, and success. Again the WHS Tigers climbed to the top of Section VII! The repeated championship brought pride to the students, administration, faculty, and community of Wilkinsburg.

WHS received another honor when the members of the news media voted Bruce Atkins (last row, #44 standing) a member of the WPIAL All Tournament Team, Class AAA. Bruce's outstanding performance at the Civic Arena made him the top vote-getter and, thus, the number one player in the WPIAL Tournament, Class AAA.

1978-79 was an exciting school year for fans of the WHS Tiger Teams!

The 1978 football team was undefeated and won a section championship for the first time since 1961. As section champions, the Tigers met and defeated Clairton in the WPIAL quarter-finals, but lost to Beaver Falls in the semi-finals. Many of the members of this championship team received individual honors. One outstanding athlete, Walter Bowyer was selected for the Suburban Conference All-Star Team, the all WPIAL Team, All-State Second Team and named one of the top 44 players in the state by the Pittsburgh Press. Another player, DeCarlos Cleveland was selected for the Suburban Conference All-Star and the all WPIAL Team.

1979 Mens Varsity basketball team

WHS advanced to the semi-finals of the WPIAL play-offs held at the Civic Arena by defeating Central Catholic 80-61 and Latrobe 57-50. The team lost to Beaver Falls 62-53 in the semi-final game. WHS then went to Indiana and was defeated by South Hills 66-61 in the first round of the state play-offs. Two members of this team received high individual honors. Walter Bowyer, forward and John Ryan, guard, were invited to play in the Akron All-American Classic and in the Cold Classic. Walter Bowyer was selected for the first team, all WPIAL Tourney Team. John Ryan was one of ten Pennsylvanians chosen to play in the Dapper Dan Roundball classic of 1979.

The "Fighting Tiger" mascot , when unmasked, was discovered to be an energetic, smiling WHS student.

1973-74 Tiger Terry Devenpeck

1971-72 Tiger Nanet M. Hamlin

Tiger explains the facts of life.

1987 Tiger - Kirk Womack

1976-77 Tiger - Vicki Rosemeyer

Tiger Pride

1983-84 Tiger

1982 Tiger

Project SCOPE and Forbes Road East were part of the WHS experience.

 In 1989   **Project SCOPE**, Student Career Opportunities and Placement Experience, was operated through the Allegheny Intermediate Unit. Participating students were prepared to successfully enter the job market. As a part of the program, eleventh grade members were given an opportunity to participate in a ten week job experience.

        Students from WHS have the opportunity to attend **Forbes Road East Vocational Technical School**. Every morning, these students travelled to Monroeville to participate in their specialized courses. Courses included carpentry, electrical, dental assisting, computer programming, beauty culture, and others. In the afternoon, students returned to WHS for their regular classes. Many Forbes Road students were able to find immediate employment because of their special training. These students were in the 1988-89 program.

Future Business Leaders of America

A new program instituted by the FBLA was the Tiger's Den, the school store. In its first months of operation in 1970 it was wholly managed by FBLA. Later, other clubs were given a chance to run the store and share in its profits. In 1971-2, for the first time, boys were allowed to join the club. Together they worked on the Tiger's Den, Christmas candle sale, bowling party, Children's Hospital Tag Day and Betty Crocker Coupon collection for the prevention of drug abuse in coordination with Teen Challenge.

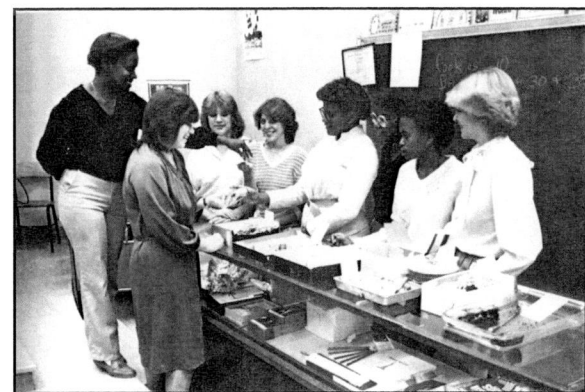

These photo images were all taken in the late 1970s and 1980s.

1982 Tiger themed T-shirt sales

1979 Tiger poster for sale in the Tiger's Den

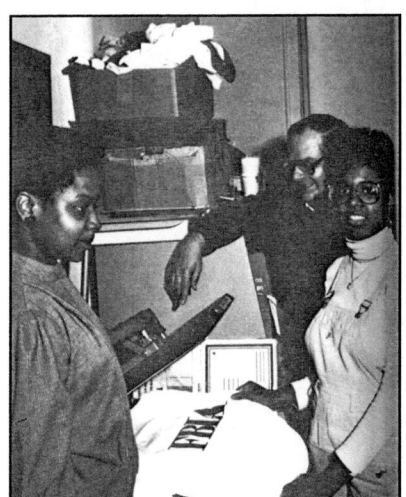

FBLA members produced and sold sweatshirts to raise money. Other FBLA clubs in Pennsylvania purchased the sweatshirts from WHS members. This image shows the 1986-1987 FBLA club.

Wilkinsburg High School has always had a strong Science Department.

1970 Physics class

1986 Biology class

Early 1980s Chemistry class

1989 Chemistry class

In 1970 WHS senior Bob Stacy, an Honors Student received the Rensselaer Award .

WHS teachers took great interest in the students.

Mrs. Sutyak's study skills lab, 1989

Principles of color, 1989

Mr. Schnur's German class, 1989

Desks rearranged to facilitate discussion, 1982

Honor Society members showed that they were academically minded.
These were members of the 1988 Honor Society.

WHS faculty members filled multiple roles and set records in employment longevity.

Music Department teachers stayed at WHS for many years developing student talent.

Jerry Shannon
Choir Director
1964 - 1971

Theodore Robins
Music Dept. Head and
Orchestra Director
1955-1981

Richard Camp
Band Director
1950 to 1970 and
Personnel Director
1970-1976

Louise Lugar, William Balawajder
Mrs. Lugar was Choir Director
1981-1993 then Band Director
1993-1995
Mr. "B" was Band Director from
1970-1993, then 1995-2003

Mr. William Lohr served as Principal, football coach,
and math teacher at WHS from 1945 to 1973.
This image was taken in 1972.

Department Heads of Wilkinsburg High School, 1973-74

Standing: Mr. Theodore Robins, Mr. Eugene Rotonto, Mr. Gerald Hebert, Mr. Edward Little, Mr. Walter P. Miller, Mr. James Garzia, Mr. Walter Smith, Mr. Clement DeFrancesco, Mr. Merlin Chute, Mr. Clarke T. Miller
Sitting: Miss Patricia Lindstrom, Mrs. Rebecca Fest, Mrs. Patricia Jones, Mrs. Mary Pasculle, Mrs. Margaret Neri

Mr. Clarke T. Miller, who retired as head football coach in the fall of 1972, coached at WHS for seventeen years. Under his direction the Tiger Football Team won the WPIAL Class AA title in 1957 and reached the finals in 1961. Mr. Miller's strong leadership led the Tigers to many victories. Mr. Miller's dedication and service as our football coach will always be recognized as a major part of WHS history.

Mr. Merlin M. Chute, a 1927 graduate of WHS taught business education and recordkeeping. Mr. Chute taught at WHS for 38 years and retired in 1974.

WHS students were committed to community involvement, and the community was committed to WHS.

Key Club, an organization sponsored jointly by WHS and the Kiwanis Club, was made up of students who wished to improve WHS and the community through service projects. Some of the projects completed during the 79-80 year were: assisting with heart screening, selling refreshments at the Kiwanis Band Festival, and selling Christmas trees. The highlight of the year for Key Club members was hosting the state convention held at Seven Springs. The co-advisers of this active club were James B. Richard and William Chessman.

In 1980 Key Club members were our school's link to the community.

The **Annual Staff** went out into the community, working many hours seeking advertising patrons. This dedicated group in 1984 secured almost 60 advertisements from local businesses. They also asked family and friends to support the Annual with messages to the graduates. Patrons could support the yearbook at the Gold, Silver or Bronze levels. There were about 120 of these 'Congratulations' and 'Good Luck' messages which helped to finance the production of the 1984 Annual.

WHS students gave their best efforts to the community of Wilkinsburg.

Concerned Students Club of 1988-1989.

Concerned Students is a voluntary organization which works closely with the Student Council. Its purpose is to provide a forum for the expression of concerns about the school and the community.

In the spring, the Concerned Students held bake sales to benefit a charity. The group co-sponsored with Student Council a canned goods drive for the Wilkinsburg Community Ministry and a blood drive for the Central Blood Bank. Students and faculty members together donated thirty units of blood.

Wilkinsburg rang with music!

Vocal music director Jerry Shannon led practice with the choir

Director Richard Camp led band practice.

Wilkinsburg residents were reminded to get ready for the "sound of music" within the community. The annual Music Festival, sponsored by the Wilkinsburg School District was a three day musical event every May. More than 900 children participated in the musical extravaganza in the early 1970s. Richard L. Camp was the music supervisor for the district. The first night of the gathering was Orchestra Night. Wilkinsburg was one of the few remaining districts that included orchestra, specifically instruction in stringed instruments in the school music program. Vocal music was performed the second night of the festival. Jerry K. Shannon, director of vocal music, led choruses including the senior high girls' chorus and the A Cappella Choir. The third and final night was Band Night which included the Senior High School Tiger Band as well as the junior high and elementary bands. Assisting Director Camp with conducting duties was Theodore Robins, instrumental music teacher.

Future Business Leaders of America played an important role in the life of WHS by giving its members the opportunity to improve and widen their business skills. In 1988-89 FBLA member Heather Williams was elected to the position of Western District Representative for 1989-1990. In this capacity Heather represented WJSHS on a local, state and national level.

Quill and Scroll, the international honorary society for high school journalists, was founded in 1926. Membership in Quill and Scroll recognizes and rewards individual achievements in the field of journalism. These 1970 WHS students were chosen for the local chapter of Quill and Scroll because of their outstanding service and contributions to the Annual or HiWays.

Linda Messer, Eleanor Chute, Joe Ryan and Linda King were honored with membership in Quill and Scroll for superior work in journalism.

Membership into the **National Honor Society** is one of the highest honors that the school can confer upon any student. Eligibility requirements are character, leadership, service, and to be enrolled in the upper third of the class. National Honor Society members worked on various school and community activities. They acted as guides for visitors during Open House, collected Christmas cards for overseas distribution, assisted with Tiger hat sales, and began a school-community interaction group. Their projects included upgrading the school's image within the community.

National Honor Society members in 1971-72

Clubs and Organizations

Clubs are truly high spots in Wilkinsburg High School. They provide opportunities to try out abilities in organizing, directing, and cooperating. They are entertaining as well as instructing, giving additional information about the subject in which the students are particularly interested. There is a club to meet the requests of almost every student, as language, science, art, and books. In addition to the informative side of clubs, there is also the social side. There are games, skits, singing and dancing. Whether instructive or entertaining, students always enjoyed themselves at the meetings, and judging from the large membership, the clubs have become one of the popular high spots in WHS.

Art Club was a group of talented students who worked under the guidance of their sponsor to contribute beauty to the school and the community. The members of the Art Club created a nature mural for the Boys' Club, displayed art exhibits in the halls and helped to beautify the school with super graphic paintings. In addition to these projects, the members of the Art Club designed programs and brochures for other organizations and clubs at WHS.

Forensics Team met each weekend throughout the year to compete in speech and debate tournaments. The goal of the members was to qualify for the National Debate Tournament by becoming an effective and influential speaker in the local tournaments. The WHS team was a member of the National Forensic League and the Pennsylvania High School Speech League.

Key Club, sponsored jointly by the Kiwanis Club and the school, is an organization of students involved in community and school service work. Among the many past projects undertaken by the members of the Key Club were: selling refreshments at the Kiwanis Band Festival, tagging for the Wilkinsburg Civic Symphony Society, helping at the Boys Club, selling Christmas trees, continuing the Buddy Program at Johnston School, caroling at the Veterans' Administration Hospital, and conducting a newspaper drive in conjunction with the recycling effort. Members of Key Club attended the Pennsylvania District Convention at Seven Springs to compete for various service and achievement related awards. Membership in Key Club is truly the "key" to success for many students at WHS.

Student Council served as a link between the student body and the administration. The members were responsible for the publication of the Student Handbook, Spirit Week, school elections, the annual homeroom decorating contest, suggestion boxes, and many other activities and projects including the Concerned Students Organization. Student Council is made up of representatives from each of the four upper classes at WJSHS. Its major goals are to provide leadership and school spirit for the entire student body. The highlight of the fall season was a traditional Wilkinsburg Spirit Week. The week of fun activities included club day, class day, dress-up day. Spirit Week was capped by a rousing pep rally and a Tiger win at the Homecoming game.

Quotation Squad brightened WHS bulletin boards. Helpful and thought-provoking quotes placed on all homeroom bulletin boards throughout the year were the result of the consciencious work of the Quotation Squad. They were very effective in enriching our school.

Since 1931 WHS seniors have marched across Graham Field to receive their diplomas.

Few things about graduation have changed over six decades. The students march through a lattice arbor, just as they did in the early 1930s.

The graduation caps and gowns are still worn, but are no longer basic black. The gowns for the girls are red and the boys wear blue, the school colors of WHS.

Families come to watch the awarding of diplomas, seniors feel mixed emotions as they leave behind their high school days. Graduation day has come!

Principal Joseph Tindal addressed the graduates and their families at commencement in 1987.

Graduating seniors in 1989 were ready for Commencement, in the last important school event of the decade.

Chapter 7 - Pride, Progress and Partnerships, 1990-2010

In the 1990s parents had more educational choices than ever. Students in Western Pennsylvania, including Wilkinsburg, could attend Catholic/Christian religious schools, internet 'cyber' schools, 'home' schools, charter schools, or the local public school. These choices, along with smaller family size and a generally decreased population in the Pittsburgh area, shrank the number of students attending Wilkinsburg Schools.

In a continuing effort to provide quality education while being fiscally responsible, WHS engaged in a number of partnerships. With the rich educational resources of local universities, WHS was able to access these resources and share in new educational techniques and technologies. The school also invited many experts in their fields to come and share knowledge with WHS students.

In 1992 students made banners to welcome state legislators
Representative Ron Cowell and Representative Joseph Preston to WHS.

Rep. Ron Cowell spoke to students in their classrooms.

Partnerships with Pittsburgh-area universities and resources enhanced the 1990s.

Senior Christopher Franciscus served a student internship at the Pittsburgh Zoo, in connection with the WHS Gifted Program in 1990. Student roles at WHS are never limited to the classroom alone.

Many activities help to prepare students for the world of work after graduation. School-Community Day is a perfect example of the varied activities students take part in. Seniors enjoyed reversing roles with district personnel for a day. Band members and cheerleaders practiced long hours to participate in a parade on Penn Avenue. Students also painted signs, made nametags, led building tours and hosted the luncheon. Student involvement was at an all-time high. This view was in 1992 when students met with Wilkinsburg's police department.

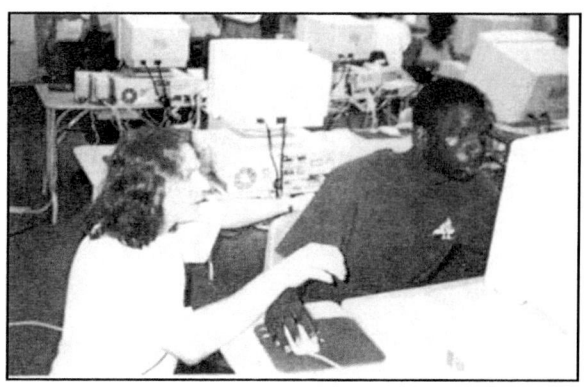

In 1998 Summer GISEP (Geographical Information System Education Program) continued at WHS. In the left image Carnegie Mellon Graduate Assistant teams with WHS teacher Mr. Schnur for a Web Page Tutorial. In the right image Carnegie Mellon "web page" instructor assists student Dave Jones.

University of Pittsburgh Partnership increased WHS' efforts to provide quality education.

Dr. Scheinberg, Dr. Norman Randolph, Mr. Ferguson, Dr. Wilma Smith (U. of Pgh.) Mrs. Martin-Carr, and Mrs. Jones confer with representatives from the University of Pittsburgh.

Hail to Pitt In 1995 the staff of the University of Pittsburgh's Panther Prints Yearbook helped the WHS yearbook staff. Many thanks to Pitt for helping to get the yearbook assembled on the computer. These views are of the WHS yearbook staff working on their copy.

Key Club continues to be a vibrant part of the school-community bond. These are members of the 2003 Kiwanis Key Club. Key Club members became involved in collections for needy families, recycling in environmental programs, community clean-up, and Boy's Club partnering.

WHS students win big at Innovative Design Contest at the University of Pittsburgh.

The Science Olympiad is an international organization devoted to improving the quality of science education, increasing student interest in science and providing recognition for outstanding achievement by both teachers and students. The program is designed to involve students in scientific inquiry. At WHS, these goals are accomplished through classroom activities, research, training workshops and participation in regional tournaments.

WHS contest winners are, (left to right) Monsae' Jones, Tisha Harris, the late Jason Paylor, Jalisa Fields, Alexandra Porter and Frenchie Skeffery. Their teachers and advisors are, (left to right) Lawson Shaw, Jim Bilka, and Rick Domm.

Two teams of WHS students attained Best Innovation honors in the University of Pittsburgh's fifth annual Innovative Design Competition held in 2010 at Soldiers and Sailors Memorial Hall. One of those teams also went on to achieve Best Design and second place overall, along with $2,000 scholarships and paid summer internships at the University of Pittsburgh. In honor of their achievement, all winning students were presented with medals and Einstein Awards for Innovation.

The High School Innovative Design Competition engages students as both scientists and engineers, charged with the task of designing creative solutions to difficult problems. In the field of physics, juniors Frenchie Skeffery and Monsae' Jones, led by teacher Jim Bilka, won Best Design, Best Innovation, and overall second-place for their design of an artificial limb called The Cloud Nine. The Cloud Nine enables its user to apply a gripping force to an object that needs to be lifted or moved. Frenchie and Monsae' also received $2,000 scholarships and paid summer internships in Pitt's John A. Swanson Center for Product Realization.

In the field of Chemistry, sophomores Alexandra Porter, Jason Paylor, and Tisha Harris, along with junior Jalisa Fields, won first place in Innovation and Best in Science for their design of a cooling system for the bullet-proof vest. Their motivation came from knowing that such vests have been proven to raise body temperatures to unhealthy levels. Led by teachers Rick Domm and Lawson Shaw, the team plans to partner with the local police department to put the Cooling Off Protective System to use.

Monsae' Jones and Frenchie Skeffery display their award from Pitt.

High schools who participated in the competition include: Woodland Hills, McKeesport, North Catholic, Steel Valley, and Westinghouse.

School-sponsored activities continue to happen.

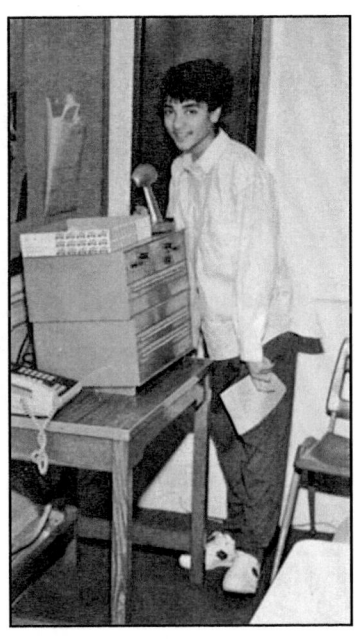

In 1990 Principal Dr. Norman Randolph instituted daily public address announcements written and delivered by students to the entire school.
In this image, student LaDonna Morton greeted classmates with early morning announcements

With a federal grant, Wilkinsburg's 21st Century After-School Program offerings include the Top Notch recording studio where students learn to make their own CD's.

The College Club's mission at WHS is to encourage and direct students to pursue a higher education. To achieve this, visits to area colleges and tours to historically Black Colleges and Universities, 17 total schools, were taken. Students meet regularly to chart their school progress in academics and college requirements. These students are members of the 1997 College Club.

The Wilderness Program was started in 1996 by the Student Forum and was sponsored by Mr. Thomas Rostek. The Wilderness Program had activities that taught members about the great outdoors. The students looked forward to their overnight camping adventures. Through these activities, members learned how to work together to survive. They find out that they have the strength to make it, not only in the wilderness, but in this world as well.

Science, chemistry, physics, mathematics all were part of the curriculum of disciplined minds

1994 Mr. Hilliard teaches a math class at WHS

Science students use microscopes in their advanced classes.

In 1996 a WHS student enjoys his chem studies.

1994 Mr. Thomas Rostek teaches chemistry

1994 Mr. Gbur reviews the periodic table of elements.

Students are encouraged to explore new technology.
By the 2000s the school was completely wired for the internet.

In 1999 WHS had computer labs with internet access.

In 2003 WHS had a number of laptop computers for added portability.

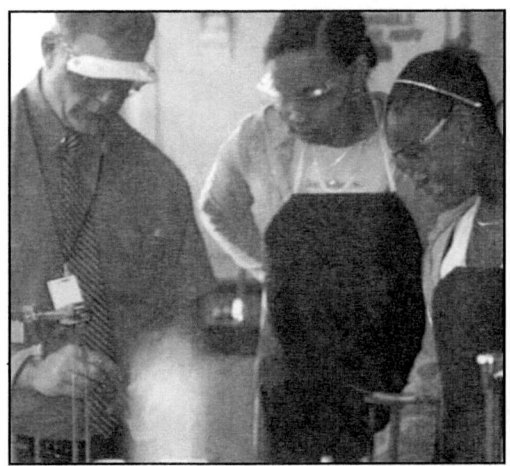

Mr. Domm works with chemistry students in this 2004 image.

Students pay attention in home economics class in these 1989 images.

Mrs. Rupani used flashcards for a Spanish lesson in this 1991 image.

Ms. Gassette, in 1991, taught principles of design.

Graham Field continues to be the land of excitement in Wilkinsburg!

The 1997 boys and girls track teams had a great season. At the WPIAL finals, the Wilkinsburg Tigers captured 1st place in the 100 meter dash, 2nd in the 200 meter dash, 4th in the 400 meter dash and 2nd in the 400 meter relay. As a result, Wilkinsburg qualified 6 people to go to the state finals. In 1999 Chaz Clemons was the state champion in both the 100 meter and 200 meter dashes. Chaz is on the far right, first row.

Wilkinsburg's Tiger mascot turned 80 years old in 2009. The Tiger was adopted in 1929 as the symbol of the spirit of WHS.

Pep Club was a relatively new organization at WHS in this 1990 photograph. The members assisted the cheerleaders in making athletic events more lively occasions. They attended all home and many away games. Their fundraising activities enabled them to buy distinctive sweatshirts which were worn to the games.

Wilkinsburg football players and cheerleaders are still in focus.

1996 Tiger football team under coach Tony Mitchell worked hard during a year of rebuilding. Three members of the team were named to the WPIAL Class A All Conference Team: Emanuel McClendon #89, Antwan Nelson #55, and Andre Williams #59.
Also in the picture is Lance Logan #30 and Bert Smith #64.

Wilkinsburg wins No. 500! On September 25, 2010 the Tigers earned their 500th win in school history, beating host Our Lady of the Sacred Heart, 26-21, at Robert Morris.

Wilkinsburg was the 18th team in WPIAL history to win 500 games.

The 1999 WHS Cheerleaders practiced year-round to promote school spirit at football games, pep rallies, and basketball games. During the summer the girls attended cheerleading camp at Slippery Rock University to prepare for the "98-99" season. There, Captain Aja Gaddie (middle kneeling) won the National High School Cheerleading All-Star Award; with this award Aja obtained the opportunity to represent Wilkinsburg in London, England.

The late 1990s brought out stellar talent in WHS boys sports.

In 1998 WHS boys basketball varsity record was 17-7 and junior varsity record was 19-2. Excitement reigned on November 28th in the Ford City Tip Off Tournament when Wilkinsburg brought home the first place trophy.

Julian Sparrow was named to the All Tournament team and Anthony Alexander won the tournament MVP.

1999 Varsity Boys Team

1999 Varsity Boys Team co-1st place AA WPIAL Division Champs.

The Varsity Boys Tiger Basketball Team had a great season in 1999. They finished with only three defeats in the regular season. The Tiger Basketball team made it to the second round of playoffs.

1998 WHS Football team

The Tigers capped off their most successful season in two decades by posting an 8-3 record and winning by an average of 15 points per game. They advanced to the second round of the WPIAL playoffs. For the second time running back #5 Laron Moore was selected "1st Team All Conference". Center Leroy Hall was also selected "1st Team All Conference". Tony Mitchell (front row, far right) was the Tiger's head coach.

The Tigers and Lady Tigers basketball teams were often winners.

2002 Men's basketball team had a perfect season, 24-0, of course winning their section. In the first round it was Wilkinsburg 55, Riverside 42 and in the quarterfinals WHS 77, Neshannock 62. In the semifinal Beaver Falls 74, Wilkinsburg 65 in overtime.

Wilkinsburg's 2003 Lady Tigers basketball team had an outstanding season, giving them a section championship.

Jaquaylla Kessler holds a Lady Tigers basketball commemorating her career 1000th point on December 11, 2006.

In 2008 the Tigers basketball team became Class A, Section IV Champs, with an 8-0 record in their section. The team finished their year in the second round of the PIAA state-wide playoffs. Coaches were Odell Miller, John Minor and Dennis Rockwell.

Alumni members and the Pittsburgh Symphony Orchestra are honored.

WHS honored some of its most outstanding alumni with a "Wall of Fame" in January, 2010. From left to right they are: Thomas Douglas, Carnegie Mellon music professor; John Thompson, Mayor of Wilkinsburg; James B. Richard, former Wilkinsburg Tax Collector and District Justice; Valerie McDonald Roberts, Manager of Allegheny County's Department of Real Estate; and brothers Livingstone M. Johnson and Justin M. Johnson, both retired Judges. The purpose of the Wall of Fame is to honor our past graduates, whose numerous and varied successes are worthy of emulation by our younger generations. The Wall of Fame was established by the WHS Student Council.

The Pittsburgh Symphony Orchestra (PSO) has presented Community Engagement Concerts in the WHS auditorium for eight consecutive years, beginning in 2003. This image shows that first PSO concert along with a local citizens choir.

In November 2010 PSO Assistant Conductor Thomas Hong lead the Orchestra in a program featuring violinist Gareth Johnson, senior division winner of the 2010 Sphinx Competition. The PSO's Community Engagement Concerts in Wilkinsburg have raised more than $53,000 since their inception. All ticket proceeds from the concerts in Wilkinsburg continue to benefit the Wilkinsburg School District's music programs.

Kings, Queens, and royal courts were highlights of Homecoming and Prom.

WHS 1992 prom court, with the King, Queen and their attendants

2004 Homecoming King and Queen

Prom Committee was a group of senior students and parents who discussed plans and promoted fundraising projects for the big event. The outcome of their efforts were successful proms held in mid-May every year.

1990 homecoming royal court

2003 prom court

2008 Homecoming King, Raymon Howell and Queen, London Johnson,
with Superintendent Archie Perrin and Principal Ella Rawlings

Commencement will always be the high point for every WHS student.

1991 seniors are just steps away from receiving their diplomas.

1991 graduating senior Kelly Cain led her class in singing the Alma Mater.

In 1992 due to inclement weather the Commencement was held in the WHS auditorium.

Valedictorian and Salutatorian of 2002 wear their gold honor cords.

1992 seniors moved their tassels, signifying that they are now graduates.

The class of 2003 waits to receive their diplomas.

Chapter 8 - The next century begins - 2011

The citizens of Wilkinsburg look confidently to the future. Currently, in the year 2011, the school district serves about 1625 students. Wilkinsburg is now surrounded by the school districts of Pittsburgh, Penn Hills, and Woodland Hills, which are three of the largest in Allegheny County and among the largest in the state. The Wilkinsburg community and the 2011 Board of School Directors retain the same firm commitment to education as did the settlers who came to the area over 150 years ago.

2011 Board of School Directors
Left to right seated:　Donora Craighead, Raymond Griffith, Jerome Garrett, Sr.(Vice President), Jean Dexheimer.
Left to right standing: Karen E. Payne (President), Carole J. Lee, Barbara Thompson,
Archie D. Perrin (Superintendent), Nanet Hamlin-Black, LaTonya Washington

This commitment to education will be further enhanced with the mentoring program, where each 11th grade student is assigned to at least one mentor in the school that will stay with them the entire school year to help guide them academically and socially. The mentors consist of teachers, administrators, specialists, and qualified support staff in the high school who check-in weekly face-to-face with their students. This is done to review student progress, develop action plans, and establish mutual accountability amongst the mentor, student, teachers, and family. Mentors are teachers who understand and are available to the students.

The district continues to provide a vast array of programs to serve the needs of the students and the community. An experienced and dedicated staff has access to the latest materials and technology to prepare our young people for the future.

Additionally, the community remains a center for commerce and transportation. With the Martin Luther King Busway, the business district is still vibrant. There is also a firm commitment by Pittsburgh History and Landmarks to the Wilkinsburg area. Application has been made to PHLF for a historic landmark plaque to be placed on Wilkinsburg High School to confirm its importance as a significant part of local history.

WHS is viewed by satellite from outer space!

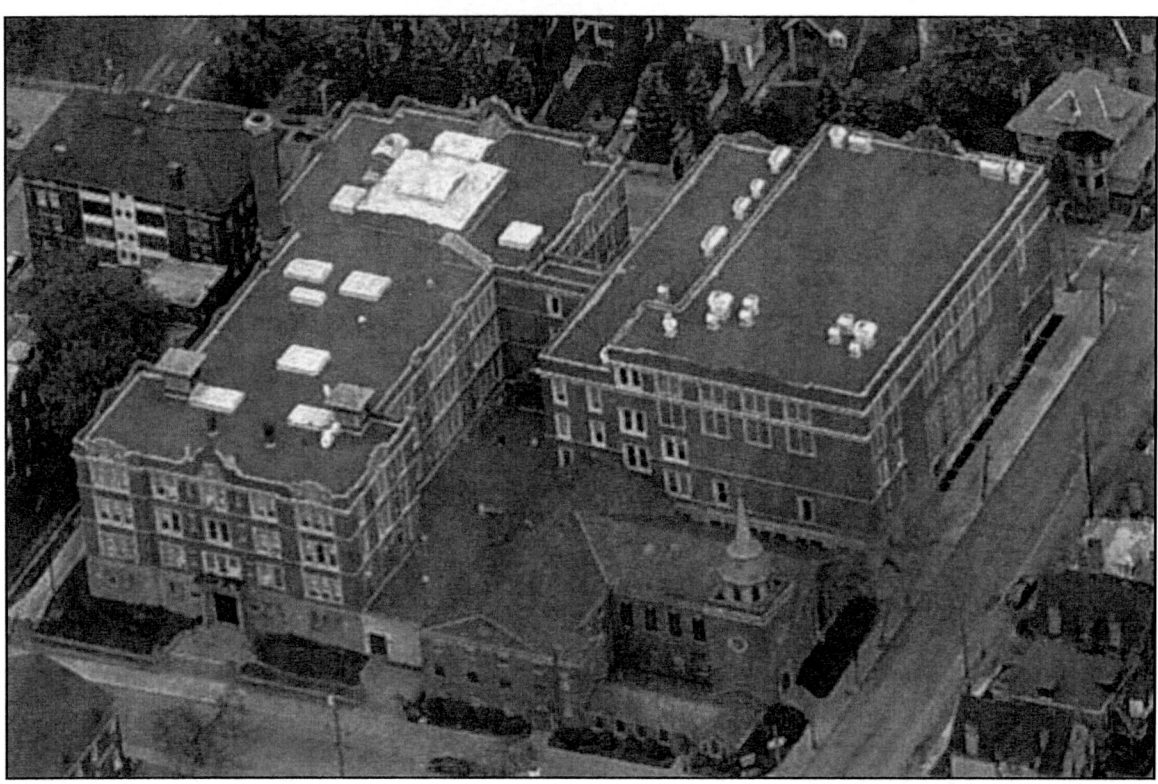

One hundred years ago Wilkinsburg students canvassed the borough, petitioning citizens to vote for construction of a high school building. The School Board approved the plan and on March 30, 1911 the beautiful Wilkinsburg High School was dedicated. The 1911 Board, faculty and students could not have imagined that the future of the school would include microcomputers, satellite images, and other technologies of the new millenium.

Just as those early educators and students did not know what the future held, the current School Board and faculty can't predict the future either. They can only continue to set high standards, work to help students achieve a quality education and encourage the community to support their efforts. The young people of Wilkinsburg <u>are</u> the future, and it is every citizen's responsibility to do their part to make that future bright.

However, with a century's worth of high school graduates behind it, Wilkinsburg High School's staff, student and parent-community stakeholders have initiated the extraordinary opportunity to engage in the Middle States Self-Study process to seek Accreditation for the Secondary School's next century of graduates. The purpose of the Accreditation process is to improve the education of youth by evaluating the degree to which the schools have attained worthwhile outcomes set by its own staffs and community. This is accomplished by undergoing a comprehensive self-assessment of the Secondary school to identify its best practices and target areas of improvement to become effective 21st Century schools of high-achieving students and an attractive anchor asset for the community of Wilkinsburg.

Accreditation is the affirmation that a school provides a quality of education that the community has a right to expect and the education world endorses. When the Middle States Commission on Secondary Schools accredits a school, it certifies that the school has met the prescribed twelve qualitative standards of the Middle States Association within the terms of the school's own stated philosophy and objectives. Standards define the level of quality required in each area of an institution's educational programs, operations, and services expected of all accredited institutions. The Standards address best practices that provide the foundations for quality and deliverance of the educational program services, activities and results in terms of student learning.

A school must meet the best practices of the twelve Standards to an acceptable degree to be granted "Accreditation" by the Middle States Association. If a Standard is not met to the acceptable level, the school must then provide an action plan for improvement to meet the Standard.

Nine Mile Run Watershed Association and WHS have partnered with Kiwanis Key Club.

"Storm Water - Swim with the high school Key Club" is a 2011 project of the Nine Mile Run Watershed Association. Key Club members will design the project under direction of the NMRWA which will be completed during the spring and summer of 2011.

With funding from the Heinz Endowments, the Nine Mile Run Watershed Association is directing the conceptual design and installation of a rain garden and green space to ameliorate the problems of stormwater runoff in a vacant lot adjacent to WHS. The WHS Key Club is working with NMRWA staff in a series of design charrettes to develop conceptual drawings for the beautification of the lot. The charrettes allow students to solve a real life problem in their neighborhood, engaging them in a creative process that also focuses on green solutions. When finished, this aesthetic example will provide residents and community members with an experience that highlights the transformation of a little used vacant lot into a valuable neighborhood asset that connects people to a more natural world.

Key Club members and NMRWA staff stand on the land that will soon become a "rain garden". Located on the west side of WHS, this garden will be another way for students to positively impact the community. Sarah Jackson (front row middle) is WHS Key Club President, Advisors to the project are Sara Madden and Lisa Brown of the NMRWA and Dominic Woods Faculty Advisor.

**As Wilkinsburg High School begins its next century,
we look forward with hope and look backward with pride.**

"We are justly proud of the record of the Wilkinsburg school system, of its scholastic, cultural, and athletic attainments, but we hope its greatest success has been in aiding to develop the characters of the young people of this community Its faculty, in the past and at present, has been faithful and unselfish in its service. Its thousands of graduates have left to us high ideals, as exemplified in our chapel and in our activities.

Much as we glory in our past, the present and the future should concern us more. Let us resolve to do everything that we can for the betterment of our community and our school."

The above words were written by William C. Graham in 1937 at the fiftieth anniversary celebration of Wilkinsburg's incorporation. Now, 74 years later his wise words are still eloquent and inspirational.